"Maybe this would be a good time to tell me what I've been doing since early February," he said.

Harper sighed. "That's a lot of memories."

There was a hitch in her voice that had him turning his head. "You okay?"

"I'm fine."

"If you say so." Lucas knew better than to push. "Anything important happen that I ought to know about?"

"I...um..." She stared straight ahead, her lips a thin line.

Lucas stared at her profile. The mahogany-brown tresses, highlighted naturally with red. Her moss green eyes, hidden behind dark sunglasses.

"Is that a no?" he asked.

Harper nodded, her gaze firmly fixed on the road.

Goose bumps ran down his arms, and his gut said something was up. They'd been friends a long time, and he knew the signs of trouble brewing. All he could do was wait it out.

Trouble was, he suspected it had something to do with his missing memories. The more he thought about what it could be, the more his head hurt.

Not good, Morgan.

Not good at all.

T0188687

Tina Radcliffe has been dreaming and scribbling for years. Originally from Western New York, she left home for a tour of duty with the US Army Security Agency stationed in Augsburg, Germany, and ended up in Tulsa, Oklahoma. Her past careers include certified oncology RN, library cataloger and pharmacy clerk. She recently moved from Denver, Colorado, to the Phoenix, Arizona, area, where she writes heartwarming and fun inspirational romance.

Books by Tina Radcliffe

Love Inspired

Lazy M Ranch

The Baby Inheritance
The Cowboy Bargain
The Cowboy's Secret Past
The Cowboy's Forgotten Love

Hearts of Oklahoma

Finding the Road Home
Ready to Trust
His Holiday Prayer
The Cowgirl's Sacrifice

Big Heart Ranch

Claiming Her Cowboy
Falling for the Cowgirl
Christmas with the Cowboy
Her Last Chance Cowboy

Love Inspired Suspense

Sabotaged Mission

Visit the Author Profile page at LoveInspired.com for more titles.

The Cowboy's Forgotten Love

TINA RADCLIFFE

LOVE INSPIRED
INSPIRATIONAL ROMANCE

LOVE INSPIRED®
INSPIRATIONAL ROMANCE

Recycling programs for this product may not exist in your area.

ISBN-13: 978-1-335-93685-1

The Cowboy's Forgotten Love

Copyright © 2024 by Tina M. Radcliffe

Love Inspired
22 Adelaide St. West, 41st Floor
Toronto, Ontario M5H 4E3, Canada
www.LoveInspired.com

Printed in Lithuania

MIX
Paper | Supporting responsible forestry
FSC® C021394

God is my strength and power:
and he maketh my way perfect.
—*2 Samuel* 22:33

Acknowledgments

Everything comes full circle. As Lucas Morgan's book ends my journey to Homestead Pass, Oklahoma, a big thank-you to Deborah Clack, who lit the flame that ignited this story idea. Thanks to Sherry Peters Photography and Bradbury Lane for the print of the Morgan boys. I am grateful.

A final thanks to reader Kim Church, who helped me research Lawton, Oklahoma.

Chapter One

Despite the heat of Oklahoma's last days of summer, Harper Reilly opened all the windows of her truck and let the hot afternoon breeze blow through the cab and whip through her hair. She turned the radio louder and grinned. Life was good.

After a lifetime of being Lucas Morgan's bestie, she might finally be moving out of the friend zone. She'd mustered the courage to tell him she cared for him three weeks ago at his brother Trevor's wedding and was nothing less than stunned when the cavalier lady's man admitted he felt the same way.

Since then, they'd been separated by rodeo circuit obligations. Friday, she'd joined him in Lawton for the Lawton Rangers Rodeo, and she couldn't stop smiling. Luc was the partner she'd prayed for. The man she longed to settle down with for whatever the future held.

Their performance at the rodeo provided a sweet preface for them to reconnect and discuss where they would go from there on a personal level. On a professional level, she had a list of important things to discuss with him regarding the training center the two of them hoped to launch next year.

Harper had placed first in cowgirl's barrel racing, and Luc had done well in saddle bronc riding, taking the number two spot after gaining ground on his competition. It was good to see his name on the leaderboard. Following a year riddled with injuries, things had begun to turn around in March. Luc had stayed on the leaderboard ever since. She couldn't be happier for him. He wanted to go out on top, and that dream was coming true.

Harper checked the dash clock. She'd left her trailer with plenty of time to head into town for Saturday dinner. She and Luc were supposed to meet at Milano's Italian Restaurant for a romantic meal. He hadn't said the word *romantic*, but she'd already checked the place out online. It was definitely romantic.

She smiled again. Was she getting ahead of herself? She hoped not.

They'd shared many meals over the years, but tonight— tonight was like a first date. The rodeo events were over, and they would have a chance to really talk. Yes, there was a lot on the line tonight and she was ready to make serious plans for the future.

As she rounded a bend in the road, the red and blue flashing lights of emergency and police vehicles glowed in the overcast sky. The chatter and intermittent static of a police radio and the crunching of tires filled the air as vehicles slowly moved past the scene on the left side of the road.

Though she couldn't tell exactly what had happened, Harper sent up a silent prayer for whoever might be involved in the mishap that had caused the two-lane road to be funneled to a single lane with traffic stopped in either direction. A police officer in an orange reflective vest waved her on, and she moved cautiously past the emergency vehicles.

Then the accident scene became visible. A truck had hit a tree. Its front fender and the hood were crumpled, and the front window was shattered.

A black Ford truck. It was a popular vehicle. Back home in Homestead Pass, all the Morgan boys had black pickups. Yet goose bumps raced down her arms, and her heart rate picked up. Harper's gaze landed on the license plate depicting a white scissor-tailed flycatcher against a blue landscape.

LAZYM#4.

Luc! The fourth Morgan sibling. The man who held her heart.

Her stomach dropped and she nearly hit the brakes. Catching herself at the last moment before she caused another accident, Harper checked her rear mirror, signaled and pulled off the road once she'd cleared the accident perimeter. She jumped from the dually and stumbled when her feet hit the asphalt. Realizing she wore heels and not her usual boots, she regained her balance and raced across the street toward the ambulance, her sundress billowing.

Two uniformed emergency medical responders loaded a person through the open rear doors just as she reached the vehicle. One of the techs climbed into the ambulance while Harper strained to get a look at the person on the gurney. All she saw was the soles of boots and an IV bag suspended on a pole swaying gently.

"My head is killing me," the patient moaned.

Harper startled at the sound of Luc's voice. Her heart clenched. This couldn't be happening.

"Wait. That's Luc," she called.

"Lady, we gotta go." The second tech stood with his hand on the door, his body effectively blocking her from getting any closer.

"Please. Is he going to be okay?"

"Are you immediate family?" he asked.

"A close friend." *Not family. I'm his almost girlfriend.*

The tech looked at his partner inside the vehicle and exchanged a silent communication. He leaned closer. "His condition is serious though stable. Your friend is confused at the moment." The tech raised a hand and met her gaze. "You didn't hear that from me, or I'll lose my job for sure."

Harper nodded. "Thank you. Which hospital are you taking him to?"

"Southwestern Medical Center. Lee Boulevard."

The door slammed and the tech jumped into the driver's seat while Harper stood on the side of the road, wrapping her arms around herself as the wind began to pick up. The faint smell of burning rubber reached her nose and she shivered. Overhead, the darkening sky had become more ominous as sirens and flashing lights escorted the ambulance toward town. The wail and yelp blared over and over until it faded out of earshot.

"Ma'am, may I help you?"

Harper whirled around at the voice. A kindly faced police officer in a blue short-sleeved uniform peered at her.

"Lucas Morgan. He's... He's a close friend."

"Ah. This must be quite a shock," the officer returned. "But he's in good hands." He stared at her for a moment. "You look familiar. What's your name?"

"Harper Reilly."

"Reilly. Barrel racer. I saw you take the big prize on Friday. Congratulations."

"Thank you." Heat warmed her face at the unexpected recognition.

"I'm sorry about your friend. Do you need directions to the hospital?"

"My truck's guidance will find it. But thank you." Harper wiped away the moisture sprinkling down on them as they stood on the side of the road.

"Ma'am, would you happen to have a number for his next of kin to notify them about the accident? I asked Mr. Morgan for that information, but he was a bit confused. Head injury and all."

Harper straightened at the words and searched the policeman's face. "Head injury?"

"That's not a diagnosis, mind you. It's what I gathered from the scene." He waved an arm at the truck. "You can see the vehicle hit a tree. Though the airbag deployed, it didn't protect him from the tree branch that shot sideways through the windshield."

Stepping closer to the truck, Harper assessed the scene. Her eyes followed the tire tracks from the road to the grassy area. She blinked at the sight of the branch and the webbing of broken safety glass and began to process what she saw. Luc had been headed for the rodeo grounds, not into town. Why? The plan was to meet at the restaurant. He'd said that he had errands to run first. Perhaps Luc finished early and thought they could take one vehicle?

Either way, assessing the angle of that tree branch, she realized that Luc was fortunate to be alive.

"Do you know what happened?" Harper asked.

"An eyewitness headed in the other direction saw a deer run in front of the truck. Your friend's quick thinking helped him avoid hitting the animal, but he lost control on the wet pavement."

A horn beeped and the officer took her elbow, gently guiding her across the street. "Tow truck needs to get in here."

"Where will Luc's truck be taken?"

"To an impound lot." He pulled out a card and wrote a number on the back. "Call them on Monday."

"Thank you. I will."

Harper offered the officer the Lazy M Ranch number and turned to leave. Though she let the officer know she would be contacting the family, he'd advised he was required to call them in an official capacity as well.

Rain chased her across the road and to her truck. Hands trembling and her heart beating overtime, she fumbled with the door handle and maneuvered inside the vehicle. She wiped the moisture from her face once more then pulled her phone from her purse and hit Call on the familiar number.

The Morgan boys had suffered many losses in the past, including the death of their parents when they were young.

She'd known the family since high school. It would be better if they heard the news from her first.

"Morgan." Luc's eldest brother answered on the first ring.

"Drew, this is Harper Reilly."

"Hey, Harper. How are you?"

"I'm f-f-fine…" she stammered. "It's Luc. I'm calling about Luc." Harper stared out the window where rain tapped against the windshield, blurring the scenery.

There was an intake of breath and then silence for a moment. "Is he okay? What happened? I keep telling him it's time to retire from the rodeo."

Harper hesitated, searching for a gentle response. It wasn't fair that they had to hear the news over the phone. "A deer ran in front of his truck. He hit a tree." She swallowed. "The ambulance is taking him to Southwestern Medical Center in Lawton."

"You're in Oklahoma?"

"Yes. We finished up the Lawton rodeo this morning and planned to head to Montana for the Fallon County Rodeo tomorrow."

"You're close by. That's good. How bad is it?"

"I'm not family, so I couldn't get much information. Head injury. Serious but stable."

"You weren't with him when it happened?"

"No. Fortunately, I stumbled upon the scene as the first responders loaded him into an ambulance. They tell me he was conscious but confused."

"Okay." Drew paused as if thinking. "Okay. We'll be there right away. Thanks, Harper."

"Drew, you're two hours away, and it's raining here. Drive safely," she said. "I'll be praying."

"Yeah. Prayer. Good plan."

Harper disconnected the phone and worked to stay calm. "Lord, You've had Your hand on Luc for thirty-six years. I trust You to continue to protect him and his family. Amen."

* * *

"Harper!" Lucas waved his friend into the hospital room. Finally, he had a visitor who wasn't dressed in scrubs or a white lab coat. His best friend carried a raincoat over her arm and wore a pink floral sundress as she hesitantly stepped through the doorway and looked around the room.

"Raincoat?" Lucas asked.

"It's pouring out there." She hung her coat on the back of the door and smoothed her long, russet hair.

"Is it?" Huh. He didn't recall rain. Lucas smiled and the simple movement started off a chain reaction of pain radiating from his jaw to his temple. Pain aside, his heart warmed at the sight of his best friend in a dress, no less, and heels. Tall and willowy, she filled out the dress nicely.

"Look at you all gussied up," he said. "Got a new fella?" A spark of jealousy jumped to life, but he tamped it down. What was he thinking? Harper was his best friend. Lucas raised a hand. "Kidding. Just kidding."

Harper frowned, confusion on her face, her green eyes concerned. "Are you okay?" she asked. Worry lines marred her golden freckled complexion and concern shadowed her gaze.

"Okay? Well, that's a matter of opinion." He'd spent the last two hours being poked and questioned. All the while, his life had flashed before him on a loop. While he didn't remember the rodeo accident that had put him in the hospital, he did remember the ambulance ride. All he could think about was what a mess he'd made of things.

It occurred to him that he'd been on the circuit so long he'd missed half the important things in his life. His brothers had settled down. He'd blinked and all three of them had fallen in love with amazing women. Each of his brothers was involved in some capacity with running the Lazy M Ranch they'd all inherited when their parents died. Yep, they'd all found their path except him. Thirty-six years old, and he hadn't figured out what he wanted to be when he grew up. He wasn't any closer to finding someone to share his life with now than last year either.

"Luc?"

"Huh?" He looked at Harper. "Did you say something? Sorry. I was thinking."

"I said that I was here earlier. Your nurse told me you were getting an MRI."

Lucas scoffed. "I'm certain I've had every test there is. MRI. CT. They took a gallon of blood too." He laughed and then winced. "But you know me. I've got a hard head. I'm fine. Takes more than a mean bronc to keep me down."

"What?" She stared at him as though he had two heads instead of the one that had been knocked around in a blender.

"You know what I mean." Despite the shooting pain, Lucas laughed again. "How do you like this outfit?" He shot a disparaging look at himself in the trendy blue-and-white-patterned hospital gown and grimaced. "They won't give me my Wranglers and boots back. Believe me. I tried. I don't even know where my phone is."

"It's probably in your truck. I'll find it." She grimaced. "How are you feeling? That's quite a black eye you have. And there's a knot the size of Oklahoma on your forehead."

"Is there?" He touched the bandage at this brow line. Three stitches. The nurse in the emergency room had told him he was fortunate to not have lost his right eye. "I'm not sure what happened, but I have a wicked headache and my nose feels like I was sucker punched."

"Your nose is definitely swollen. Did they give you anything for the pain?"

"Nope. The nurse said they don't want me sedated."

He ran his fingers over the worn silver watch on his wrist. His galloping heart had settled some when he'd realized the memento, once his father's, was untouched.

"I called your brothers," Harper said.

"What?" He spit out the question and then bit back the ensuing pain. *Note to self, chill out. It hurts less.* "Why would you do that, Harp? I'll be out of here shortly, and we'll be on our way to Tucson."

"Tucson?" Her jaw sagged.

"You're still going, aren't you?" He was aware that Harper had obligations at home. The Reillys were Homestead Pass royalty thanks to Reilly Pecans, and Harper regularly pitched in during pecan harvest. Plus, her grandmother's deteriorating health had her going home often now that her folks had moved the matriarch to the Reilly ranch.

"The Tucson rodeo is held in February, Luc."

"Yep. Arizona in winter." He leaned back against the pillows and focused on that solitary cheerful thought. "I'm so ready for sunshine and saguaro cactus. Maybe we can take a side trip to Sedona again? It's out of the way, but why not? All work and no play and all that. What do you think?"

"Sedona? Let's slow down a minute here," she said. "Do you know where we are?"

Luc narrowed his eyes. Why was she asking silly questions? "I'm in Fort Worth. We've been here all week." He paused. "Are you okay, Harper? You look confused."

A disturbance in the hall had both Harper and Lucas turning toward the door. It burst open and the entire Morgan family poured into the hospital room, their boots clacking on the linoleum floor as they entered. A harried nurse followed right behind, admonishing them to be quiet before she left.

His older brothers, Drew and Sam, along with his fraternal twin, Trevor, and their grandfather all stared at him.

Lucas did a double take. Why was his entire family here?

"Well, thank the Lord," Gramps said. "You're in one piece."

"No worse for wear, as you can see. But if you're all here,

who's watching the ranch?" Lucas asked. "And how did you get here so fast?"

Gramps stepped closer to the bed with a newspaper under his arm. He pulled off his Stetson and hugged Harper. At eighty-four, Gus Morgan could easily be taken for a man ten years younger. Beneath his Stetson, his brown hair was barely touched by gray.

His grandfather turned to Lucas, the sharp blue eyes assessing. "It wasn't fast. I wanted to go south and pick up Highway 62, but Drew said the back roads were faster." Gramps scowled and rolled his eyes.

"It *was* faster," Drew said.

"My truck's suspension will never be the same," Trevor muttered.

"We took two vehicles, but your brothers wouldn't even stop for a Dr Pepper break," Gramps groused.

"What are you talking about?" Lucas asked, looking at his family. "It's four hours from Homestead Pass."

His grandfather's eyes rounded and he inched closer to the hospital bed. "In what world? It's two hours from home to Lawton."

"Lawton?" Pain surged behind Lucas's eyes as he processed what Gramps said. Then he sank back onto the pillows.

"You okay, Luc?" Trevor approached him.

"I'm fine. A little banged up, is all. I feel bad you all came out here on a Sunday."

"Sunday? It's not Sunday," Trevor said.

"Sure it is. We got into Fort Worth a week ago. That was February fifth. Do you want me to recite the alphabet backward too?"

"Easy there," Gramps said. He unfolded the paper tucked under his arm and placed it on the bed. It was an issue of the *Homestead Pass Daily Journal*. "Son, it's the middle of August. Not February. And it's Saturday night."

"What?" Lucas closed his eyes and then opened them. How could that be?

Gramps shook his head. "Mayhap, I spoke too soon. Sounds like you're having some issues with your head, son."

Lucas stared at his grandfather, trying to ignore the dizziness that threatened. For the first time since he'd arrived at the hospital, he was worried about his prognosis. How had he lost such a chunk of time? He worked to string together his memories of the events from February to now, without success. Panic simmered in his gut.

"Have you talked to a doctor?" Gramps asked.

"Talked to a couple of them in the emergency department. They asked me a bunch of questions, including what day it is, and then they sent me for tests." He shrugged, working to shake off his growing concern and his grandfather's. "I don't see what the big deal is. I've hit my head before."

Gramps shot Sam a pointed look. "Go find that nurse and tell her we want a doctor in here pronto, would you?"

"Yes, sir." His brother gave a solemn nod and left the room.

Minutes later, a different nurse rushed in. The petite young woman assessed him and then his visitors. "Dr. Gradeless will be here shortly. I apologize for the delay. He's tied up in the emergency room."

"Can you tell us what's going on with my grandson in the meantime?" Gramps asked.

The nurse looked at Lucas. "Mr. Morgan? Do you agree to share information about your medical condition with your visitors?"

"They aren't visitors. This is my family. Whatever you have to say, you can say in front of them."

Again, her gaze spanned the room. "Aside from the head laceration and bruised ribs, I can tell you that he's suffering from a concussion."

Lucas scoffed. "Is that all? I told everyone in the emergency department that I've had half a dozen of those. That's old news."

"Yes," the nurse replied. "I believe that is the doctor's concern."

A phone trilled and Harper scrambled to pull the cell from her pocket. "Excuse me. It's my father. I'll be right back."

When she slipped out of the room, the nurse gave his brothers and his grandfather a stern look. "It's past visiting hours. If you keep your voices down, you can stay until the doctor arrives. Otherwise, I'll have to speak to security and have you escorted out." She nodded and wove her way around his brothers and out of the room.

"Huh. Would never have called that," Sam said. "She looked like such a sweet little thing."

"Those are the ones you have to look out for. Trust me. I married one just like her," Trevor quipped.

"Married? When did you and Hope get hitched?" Lucas frowned, trying to sort dates in his mind without success.

"Luc, we got married on the first Saturday in August. You were my best man." Bleak concern filled his brother's blue eyes.

"Nah. Really?" Why couldn't he remember his brother's wedding? "Did I have fun?"

"You always have fun," Trevor returned. "Though, except for dancing the polka with half the church ladies, you mostly hung out with Harper."

"Could we focus here, boys? Luc here has amnesia," Gramps said. "I'm guessing there's more going on than another concussion."

"I've taken worse spills," Lucas said. That was the truth. Except this time, he didn't remember what had happened to land him in the hospital. He held up his right arm. "Remember last summer when you met your wife, Trev? Sixteen stitches up and down my arm."

"You aren't helping yourself here, Luc," Trevor muttered.

Gramps shook his head. "I don't like it. Don't like it at all." He turned to Harper, who'd entered the room again. "Sure appreciate you calling us about Lucas right away."

Harper nodded, her lips a thin line. Lucas noted the anxiety in her eyes and the tension in her slim frame. The two of them had a long history of supporting each other through the dark times and the good. He longed to hug his buddy and tell her everything would be okay.

Today, for the first time in his life, he wasn't sure everything would be okay.

The room fell silent, except for the quiet beep of the IV pump, the sound of patient call buzzers echoing from the hall and the muffled squeak of shoes on linoleum.

His brother Drew walked to the window, brow creased as he took in the night sky. Lucas hated worrying his family. The Morgans had had a rough past. Drew was the oldest, and things had fallen on his shoulders when their parents had died until Gramps moved in. Luc and Trevor had been thirteen. It hadn't been a good time, and Luc hadn't made it any easier. While his brothers were stoics who'd swallowed their grief, he had been inconsolable for over a year.

Minutes later, a light tap at the door frame proceeded the entry of a physician in a white lab coat. A tall man with a generous smile glanced around the room. "Good evening. I'm Dr. Gradeless." He took a moment to shake hands with everyone in the room and exchange introductions before approaching the foot of the bed.

Lucas tensed, his fists opening and closing as he waited for the impending diagnosis.

"Doc, what's going on?" Gramps burst out. "Luc's lost months of his life."

"I understand. The scans show a traumatic brain injury. It appears he has retrograde amnesia."

"Can you explain that so I can understand it, Doc?" Gramps asked. "What's the difference between a traumatic brain injury and a concussion?"

"A concussion is a type of TBI. The brain moves and is bruised. In your grandson's case, it's led to retrograde amnesia."

"'Retrograde amnesia,'" Drew repeated. "What can we do?"

"Rest is the most important thing right now. It's a wait-and-see situation," the doctor said. "The symptoms usually go away on their own in hours or weeks, sometimes even months."

"Wait and see?" Gramps shook his head. "No offense, Doc, but you spent all that time in medical school and that's the best you can do?"

"Point well taken." Dr. Gradeless gave a nod of acknowledgment. "Unfortunately, there is no definitive answer with head injuries. The good news is that, according to the paramedic's report, the good Samaritan who observed the crash reported that Lucas didn't lose consciousness for long. Your grandson is alert and shows no other symptoms except a headache and mild dizziness. We'll provide acetaminophen for the headache. He needs to rest for the next twenty-four hours while the staff monitors him for any worsening symptoms."

"Then I can get back to work?" Lucas ran a hand over his chin. Maybe things weren't as lousy as he'd thought.

The physician narrowed his gaze. "What work is that?"

"Rodeo. Saddle bronc riding."

"Oh no." The doctor's face reflected surprise. "That is precisely the activity you must avoid. Rest from mental and physical activity is what I'm prescribing."

Lucas stared at him, hope fading. "For how long?"

"The plan is to take things one day at a time, gradually resuming regular nonjarring activities."

"And then I'll get my memory back?"

"Once again, there are no definitive answers when it comes to a brain injury. There are various kinds of memory and a range of types of memory loss and recovery."

Dr. Gradeless eyed the group. "All of you should be observing Mr. Morgan for neurological changes as well. I'll provide a guidance handout at discharge and a referral to a neurologist in your area. He should follow up with an office visit as soon as possible, and head to an emergency room if his symptoms worsen." The doctor paused. "In the meantime, rest is the prescription."

"Rest," Lucas muttered at the offensive takeaway from the doctor's spiel.

"Think of it as an opportunity to do some of the things you've put off."

"Like what? Basket weaving?"

Gramps snorted.

The neurologist shot Lucas a disapproving glance. "Mr. Morgan, I don't think you appreciate how fortunate you are. That accident could have been fatal."

"Yeah, I'm sorry, Doc," Lucas apologized. "I know you're right, but this is an adjustment."

Dr. Gradeless scanned the room, his eyes coming back to Lucas. "Here's the best advice I can offer. Don't push yourself. If you are pressed to recall those missing memories, you're going to increase your stress and the likelihood of headaches. Additionally, that stress can lead to depression." He paused. "This isn't a race to remember the past."

Lucas stared at him, a bit stunned by the words.

"I'd like to recommend a therapist to work through how you're feeling."

Lucas nodded at Gramps. "My grandfather is the family therapist."

"Oh, I wasn't aware." Dr. Gradeless looked at the Morgan patriarch.

"He's being facetious," Gramps inserted. "But I can tell you that we're on it. Fact is, he has a sister-in-law who's a registered nurse. You can be sure he'll have plenty of care." He eyed Lucas. "Whether he likes it or not."

Lucas barely resisted groaning aloud. His gaze met Harper's. She was the one person in the room who really understood his struggles the last year. She lifted her hands as if in prayer and mouthed, *It's going to be okay.*

In that moment, he relaxed a bit. Things were messed up, all right, but he knew to keep his eyes on the Lord, no matter what. He looked at Harper again and sent up a prayer, thanking Him for his best friend.

Chapter Two

Harper stood at the foot of Luc's bed and assessed his bruised eye. The colors had transitioned from black and blue to black, blue and purple, and they stood out against the butterfly bandage that had replaced the gauze on his temple. His nose seemed somewhat less swollen and pronounced. Still, seeing the six-foot-tall cowboy in a hospital bed, wearing a blue-dotted gown and connected to an IV shook her each time she walked in the room. His wavy, caramel-colored hair could use a visit to the barber. A lock fell over his forehead and she fought the urge to push it back.

"How do you feel?" she finally asked, working to keep her voice calm and even, though she felt anything but. Last night at 3:00 a.m., while she'd stared at the ceiling of her trailer, Harper decided she would not let her own fears about Luc's memory loss and what it meant for their future take priority over his recovery. No stress, the doctor had said. Right now, it was her job as his friend to do whatever she could to be there for him. She wouldn't press him to pull up memories.

"The headache rages on." Lucas shrugged. "Got a few new aches today, including my ribs. Though my ego isn't quite as bruised now that I know a tree hit me and I didn't fall off a horse." He looked at her. "Why do you suppose I lost control of the truck anyhow?"

She studied him. Had he forgotten what she'd repeated on

Saturday and Sunday already? "The policeman said a deer ran across the road. It wasn't your fault, and there wasn't anything you could have done differently. There was a car behind you and vehicles approaching in the other lane."

"I could have *not* hit that tree. A bronc, I can understand, but a tree?"

"It was raining. Everything was slick. Cut yourself some slack."

"I guess," he muttered, his attention on the IV tubing.

Harper checked her watch. "I'm going to head over to the impound lot. I called Les Farley and someone from Farley Towing is meeting me there," she said. "They'll get your truck back to Homestead Pass."

"Harper."

She looked up and met his stare. "Thank you. I appreciate it. Thank Les for me, would you?"

"I will. Are you going to be okay until your family gets back from breakfast?"

Luc offered a bitter chuckle. "Yeah, sure. I'm surrounded by babysitters here." He nodded and then hesitated. "Thanks, Harp. You're a good friend."

A good friend. Yes, she was. Twenty-four hours ago, she'd been certain that she was moving toward more than that.

"See you back in Homestead Pass," she said.

Harper mulled over the situation with Luc as she drove to the lot. She'd hardly slept last night, tossing, and turning as she contemplated the uncertain future. All she could do was pray that his injured brain healed.

She recalled the moment everything had changed between them. It was July at the Colorado Cattlemen's Days in Gunnison. The minute his score lit up the leaderboard, Luc had raced from the arena to find Harper. He'd picked her up and whirled her around. And for the first time since they'd met, Lucas kissed her.

She lifted a hand from the steering wheel to touch her lips. *It was the sweetest kiss.*

One that made her realize that, after years content as Luc's best friend, she wanted more. Harper had been forced to admit to herself that she'd denied her feelings for Luc for far too long. Perhaps had been fearful that if things played out, one day she'd be relegated to a long line of Lucas Morgan's ex-girlfriends. She wanted it all and the kiss had given her hope maybe that wasn't a dream. After the kiss, Luc had apologized nonstop for the next twenty-four hours.

In the weeks after that, they'd pretended it hadn't happened. When she couldn't hold back any longer, she'd blurted out her feelings after Trevor and Hope's wedding. Luc's responding admission that he cared about her had knocked her boots off.

That moment was real, wasn't it? Or had he been caught up in the emotion of his brother's wedding? After seeing the tenderness in his eyes, Harper had left Homestead Pass that weekend with a full heart, and hope. Now, she wasn't certain. Had she imagined things?

The ringing of Harper's cell phone jarred her from her thoughts. The dashboard display connected to her cell flashed her father's number.

She let it go to voice mail. Harper wasn't up to another grilling. Colin Reilly had been pressing her about the family business lately. The discussions always seemed to end with a word about Luc.

Her father blamed the cowboy for turning her away from Reilly Pecans and leading her astray to the rodeo circuit.

Sure, he liked Luc. Everyone liked Luc. But he also thought he was a man without a plan. He'd told her more than once that Lucas Morgan needed to settle down, stop being a jokester, and claim his place as part owner of the very successful Lazy M cattle ranch.

Her father was wrong, Luc had a plan and once the bank

loan was approved, they'd be able to share that plan. That is, if he remembered.

Luc had a single-minded need to prove himself, and he intended to do that by opening a riding school and rodeo training facility on the ranch when he retired in January. Though she never really understood what drove Luc, she immediately knew she wanted in on the venture.

Rodeo was a young person's sport, and at thirty-two, she was already thinking about a future beyond the circuit, though she hadn't shared those thoughts with anyone but Luc.

Harper was ready for a future where she was her own boss. Not just another barrel racer or the daughter of the CEO of Reilly Pecans. She was also ready to start thinking about settling down and maybe having a family.

It had taken her months to get Luc to see past his ego long enough to convince him to let her partner with him on his plan. Come January, they'd both retire.

After all, with her skills in barrel racing and team roping, and his background and reputation in saddle bronc riding, they could combine their talent and double the potential of a training school.

Once Luc had agreed, she'd wasted no time getting the paperwork together and contacting the bank to present their strategy in hopes of funding.

They'd been turned down the first time but, unwilling to take no for an answer, and unbeknownst to Luc, Harper had resubmitted the paperwork. She'd planned to explain to Luc over dinner how she'd tweaked the financials to ensure approval this time.

The dinner that never was.

Her breath caught in her throat. Would he remember what had already been set in motion? Should she even discuss the venture with him after the doctor's warning about stress? The last thing she wanted was to endanger the healing process.

Harper slowed down as she approached the facility. Surrounded by a chain-link fence, the gated entrance to the parking lot was open. She drove through, parked, and headed to the small office.

"Hi. I'm here to pick up a truck," Harper announced.

A female clerk looked up. "Are you the registered owner?"

"No. He's in the hospital. I have a notarized letter and all the required documents. I also brought cash for the fee." Harper slid the paperwork across the counter.

"Cash. Now you're talking my language." The woman shuffled the papers, examining each one before she started typing on a keyboard. "Says here the vehicle needs to be towed."

"Yes. Farley's Towing out of Homestead Pass will pick it up today."

"The gates are locked at five sharp. If the tow isn't here and gone before then, you'll owe for another day."

"They'll be here shortly."

The clerk offered a short nod and slid the keys, attached to a tag, across the counter. "Space sixteen."

"Thank you."

The August heat radiated from the asphalt parking lot as she strode to space sixteen. Harper assessed the truck from all angles and shook her head.

Luc spent a ridiculous amount of time washing and waxing the dually, which he'd paid for in cash from his winnings last year. He was going to be one upset cowboy when he saw his baby.

In her opinion, the insurance adjuster would consider it totaled. Still, it had to be removed from the impound lot either way. Harper opened the driver's-side door wide enough to release the heat and stepped back for a moment. Then she searched for his phone beneath the driver's seat, without success.

A peek into the cab's back seat revealed his duffel, a pair of boots, a saddle and riding tack. Harper grabbed everything and put it on the ground. Luc's duffel was open, the contents a jumble of clothes scattered with glass. She'd empty the glass out before she transferred his belongings her truck.

She moved to search the passenger seat, which was also decorated with a layer of glass. She pulled a bandana from her purse and wiped the upholstery. After emptying the glove box, she carefully reached into the space beneath the center console cupholder.

Ugh. Wet carpet, an overturned disposable coffee cup and, yes, Luc's phone. His very wet phone. Harper retrieved the cell, wiped it off, and examined the cracked screen. She played with the buttons for a minute, attempting to reboot the device. When that didn't work, she removed and reinserted the SIM card. Still no sign of life.

She gave up and gathered Luc's belongings. Making several trips, she hauled his tack, boots and saddle to her truck.

At the rumble of an engine, she turned to see a Farley Towing truck enter the yard. Les Farley jump from his vehicle and look around.

"Hey, Les." Harper waved and crossed the parking lot. "Thanks for making the drive." She knew it was a big deal that Lester H. Farley himself had driven clear from Homestead Pass.

"Oh, I owe Gus Morgan more than a couple favors. This will make us about even."

As he spoke, the passenger door of the tow truck opened and a pretty blonde stepped down. When she cleared the door, Harley recognize the woman. Kit Farley Edwards. Les's oldest daughter and Harper's friend from childhood. A very pregnant friend.

"Kit?" Harper exclaimed. "You're pregnant?" Kit's was one of the many weddings Harper had attended over the last few years. It seemed everyone was getting married. Everyone but her.

Kit's smile lit up her face and she grinned with a glance at her father. "Yes. Due at the end of summer. First grandchild for my dad."

Les pushed back his worn ball cap and beamed at the words.

"Congratulations. I'm so happy for you. What are you doing back in Oklahoma?" Harper asked.

"Joe accepted a position teaching at the high school, so we packed up and left Arizona at the end of the school year."

"That's wonderful. Let me know when the baby shower is. I definitely want to attend."

"My mother-in-law will send the invitations out soon."

"Perfect." Harper frowned. "What are you doing out with your father today?"

"Joe had a training seminar, so Dad took me to Oklahoma City to pick up a crib. When the call came in, I came along for the ride."

Harper nodded. Kit had gotten married eighteen months ago and now had a baby on the way. The bliss on her face said it all, and Harper couldn't deny her envy.

"Where's Luc's truck?" Les asked.

"The black one, there all by itself," Harper said.

Les strode across the parking lot, leaving Kit and Harper alone.

"How is Lucas?" Kit asked. "His accident is all everyone's talking about in town."

"Improving. Some memory issues, but Lucas is strong and stubborn. He's on the road to recovery."

Kit put a hand on Harper's arm. "We'll be praying."

Harper nodded. The heartfelt words staved off the despair of not knowing what the future held. "Thanks, Kit."

The other woman cocked her head. "I always thought that when Luc eventually settled down it would be with you."

"I, um…" Harper swallowed, unsure what to say.

"Whoa!" Les interrupted, sparing Harper from answering her friend.

Grimacing, he removed his cap and slapped it back on his balding head. "That truck is in bad shape."

"Yes. The insurance company said someone will be out to your place to assess the damage tomorrow."

Harper handed over the keys. "I sure appreciate this, Les."

"No problem. Friends take care of each other."

Harper and Kit stood to the side as the rollback tow truck backed up to the black dually. Once Les connected the winch, it only took a short time to load the disabled vehicle and lock down the wheels.

"Looks like he's about done," Kit said.

"I'll be sure to call you now that I know you're back." Harper hugged her friend.

"Are you home for a while as well?" Kit asked.

"Probably," Harper said. She wasn't going anywhere until Luc recovered, though she wasn't sure what that looked like.

Harper's cell buzzed as she waved at the departing tow truck. She reached into her pocket and glanced at the caller ID. Gus Morgan?

"Gus. Is everything all right?"

"This is Lucas. Gramps lent me his phone. We're halfway home. I thought I'd check and see how you were doing."

Lucas.

Images of the Kit's swollen belly flashed through her mind. Longing pressed on Harper's heart.

"Harper? You still there?"

"I'm here." Her voice cracked with emotion.

"You sound sort of odd."

"Do I? No, I'm fine."

"Everything go okay with the truck?"

"Yes, Les was here, and your truck is on its way home. I grabbed all your stuff, too."

"Thanks. Any chance you found my phone?"

"I did. Unfortunately, the phone bit the bullet."

"Bummer." He sighed. "Thanks for doing all that."

The muffled sound of Gus's voice could be heard in the background.

"Gramps says he owes you Sunday dinner."

"Tell Gus thank you." She hesitated, there was so much more she wanted to ask him about what he remembered, but she held back.

"Are you sure everything is all right?"

"Yes. Of course."

"Okay, well, I have an appointment with a neurologist in Oklahoma City tomorrow afternoon. Trevor's wife pulled a few strings and got me in. Think you can take me?" He paused. "I know it's a big ask, but you're the only one who isn't making me claustrophobic right now."

"Absolutely." Asking her to help was a positive thing.

"Thank you." He paused. "It's a long drive, and I've a lot of questions. Maybe you can help me fill in the blanks on my life since February."

Harper rubbed the throbbing spot on her right temple as her eye twitched. Right now, she had as many questions as he did.

"Harper?"

"Yes. Sorry. Um, no problem. I'm sure I can help." Once again, she tried to focus on the positive. Maybe she could gently find out what he recalled about their joint venture and their relationship.

"I can always count on you, Harper. I appreciate that."

Yes, she'd be there for him, like she had dozens of times before. But, for the first time in her life, she began to question the wisdom of her devotion. Kit's words came back to her.

What if Luc would never be able to settle down? Was she destined to always be waiting for him?

The view from the front porch rocker extended all the way to the graveled entrance drive of the Lazy M Ranch and was illuminated by the full moon. Though the sun had set, the mosquitos hadn't noticed Lucas on the porch, so he continued to sit and stare into the distance.

Twice, the Good Lord had spared his life.

Why him?

He thought back to the last time he'd seen his parents alive. It had been late August then as well. His mother had been sitting in the truck, digging in her purse for her sunglasses. Lucas recalled that old pickup his father drove. He'd always said the vehicle's dents and scratches gave the old Ford personality.

Drew had graduated from college and had been working full-time on the ranch. Sam, then seventeen, had spent most of his summer working with a new horse. Trevor had been at junior high football practice that particular day.

Lucas hadn't made the cut for football and the endless months of July and August had been filled with long days helping on the ranch.

"Are you sure you don't want to come with us?" his father had asked Lucas one last time. "We're getting ice cream in Elk City. You could use a treat."

"No. I'm gonna stay and watch Sam practice. He promised to let me ride that mare he's training."

"Okay, but you wear a helmet. You hear?"

"I will." Excitement rushed through Lucas as he'd started for the corral. Then he remembered the watch his father had lent him this morning. Lucas had turned and called to his father, "I didn't give your watch back."

"Keep it for now. I'll collect it from you later."

Lucas had grinned. "Thanks, Dad. Love you."

"Back at you, kiddo."

His father'd waved and his mother had blown a kiss as the truck tires crunched over the gravel, and rumbled down the drive, leaving a wake of dust behind.

Lucas bowed his head and sighed. A deep ache crushed his

chest, nearly sucking the air from his lungs as it always did when he remembered that day. He could barely swallow past the pain that was still so raw after all these years.

Why, Lord?

The creak of the screen door startled him and he turned his head to see Gramps standing on the porch, his hip on the rail.

"What are you doing out here in the dark?" his grandfather asked.

"Thinking."

"Easy there. That doc said no strenuous activity."

Lucas chuckled. "Ever think about a second career as a standup comic, Gramps?"

"Pshaw. Not nearly as much fun as harassing you and your brothers."

They were silent for minutes; the only sounds that of the ranch at night. The cattle bellowed as a horned owl hooted to the humming white noise of the air conditioner unit.

"What's out there that has your interest?" Gramps asked.

"Thinking about the folks." He paused. "Gramps, how did you make it through that time? You lost your only child. How were you so strong?"

"We were all strong in the Lord, Luc."

"No." Lucas shook his head. "I wasn't. I cried myself to sleep for a solid year.

"No shame in that." He put his hand on Lucas's shoulder. "The Lord gave me a job to do. Didn't mean I forgot my son." Gramps tapped his heart. "I carry him in here. Then and now."

Once again, silence stretched. Then Gramps gave a slight smile. "Remember how your daddy could laugh?"

Lucas nodded, finding himself smiling. "Yeah. Dad laughed until he was short of breath. I do remember that. I've forgotten lots of things, but I'll never forget that."

"There you go. Your daddy is with you. And someday we'll

all be reunited." His grandfather pinned him with his gaze in the semidarkness. "What's eating at you?"

"I want to make Dad proud, and I feel like I'll never get there." The words spilled out of him in a rush.

"You're thirty-six. What's the hurry?"

"Gramps, my brothers have already made something of themselves. This accident has made my path to where God wants me so convoluted, even I'm not sure where I'm headed." Lucas made a face, thinking about the training school he'd hoped to open next year. A training school in honor of his father.

"All you gotta do is keep your eye on your Maker, son. I learned a long time ago not to put boundaries on what God can do in my life."

"Am I?"

"Sure you are. This accident don't mean nothing in the grand scheme of things."

There was silence between them for minutes, though the katydids continued to fill the night.

"Gramps, do you ever think things would have been different if I'd gone with them that day?" Luc finally asked.

His grandfather sucked in a breath and stumbled a step. "Playing what-if is a bad idea." Gus turned and stared at him.

"They wanted me to go. Maybe I could have done something."

"There's nothing you could have done, son. It was a drunk driver. Plain and simple." He shook his head, suddenly looking his eighty-four years. "All this time, you've had that bottled up inside you?"

"Hitting that deer. Losing my memory. Realizing I slipped by death again… It's made me think about my life. Why was I spared?" Lucas shrugged. "If He has a plan, I want to get things right."

"Relax. You're doing fine. Just keep taking the next step.

You'll get to where He wants you to be if you keep listening to that still-small voice."

"I sure hope so, Gramps. I sure hope so."

"Getting late, and I need my beauty sleep," his grandfather said.

"I'll be in shortly. I have an early morning as well. Harper is driving me to OKC for my neurology appointment."

"We're blessed to have Harper in our lives. Hope you know that."

Lucas cocked his head to look at his grandfather. "Why do you say it like that?"

"Like what?"

"Like I'm two cans short of a six-pack."

Gramps chuckled. "You said it, not me. Don't overlook what's right in front of your eyes, Lucas."

The door bounced softly and creaked again before it closed behind Gramps.

Lucas stared into the distance once again, mulling his grandfather's parting words. Right in front of his eyes?

He eased up from the chair. Yeah, he was blessed to have Harper Reilly in his life. He'd never take his best friend for granted.

"I really appreciate you taking me to this appointment." Lucas gingerly pulled on his seat belt, careful not to disturb his healing ribs. He looked over at Harper in the driver's seat of her truck and shrugged. "Not sure why there's such a rush to get me in here. This doctor didn't tell me anything new. I'm supposed to come back in two weeks. That'll be September."

"Great. I can take you if you stop thanking me." She glanced over her shoulder, signaled, and pulled into traffic.

"I can't help it. I'm grateful." He released a breath of frustration. "And I don't know why I can't drive. It's an hour and forty-five minutes each way. I hate inconveniencing you like this."

"Luc, you have to take this seriously. You've had a traumatic brain injury. What if you're driving and you have vision issues? Or a seizure?"

"Oh, I'm taking it seriously. All I can think about is that I can't remember over six months of my life and can't get on a horse." He heaved a sigh. Life as he knew it was officially over.

"This is only temporary," Harper said.

"Harper…" His voice dropped. "It's possible it could be permanent. I may never remember, and I might never get medical clearance to return to the circuit."

When she didn't answer, he looked over at her. Harper's hands were tight on the steering wheel and her face had paled.

"I'm sorry," he murmured.

"Why are you apologizing? You haven't done anything wrong," she said.

"I'm whining." He sighed again. "Nobody likes a whiny cowboy."

"Did the doctor say anything encouraging?"

"I guess. We talked about what I can do." He began to count on his fingers. "I can help Trevor with the Kids Day Event. I can paint and work in the garden. Fishing is allowed. Oh, and I can bake." He laughed and then groaned at the pain it caused. "Is that hilarious or what?"

His high-octane life was no more, and now he was reduced to baking cookies. He'd cry if the situation weren't so laughable.

"That's all he said?"

"He said I might experience emotional outbursts." Lucas chuckled. "Would this qualify as an emotional outburst?"

Harper's lips twitched. "Nope. You'll have to try harder." She shot him a quick glance.

Lucas nearly laughed out loud. Harper would let him vent,

but she wasn't going to help him throw a pity party. And she was right. That would get them nowhere fast.

"How's the headache?" she asked.

"Comes and goes. Currently present. Doc said it could last up to a year or longer." He looked at her. "More good news, right?"

"You're alive and in one piece. That would be the good news."

"Yeah. One piece," Lucas murmured. "One piece who's missing more than half a year of his memories and has no idea what he's going to do with the rest of his life. I knew I was heading toward retirement, but this wasn't how I saw things shaking out. There's no way I can start a rodeo training school in my current condition. As it stands, I've been barred from riding a horse."

"You don't have to do it alone. I'm here."

"We already talked about that. You're a rising star. You can't retire now. Besides, I want to do this without you propping me up." Without anyone propping him up, for that matter. People had coddled him ever since his folks died. He'd started on the circuit to prove himself. Lucas felt the same way about the training school.

"Luc, I'm retiring in January. Period. I may hit the circuit in my spare time, but I'm ready for the next chapter of my life."

"Since when?"

"Since we already discussed this."

"We have?"

"Let's change the subject for now. Okay? The doctor said not to push yourself to recall."

He glanced over at Harper. Once again, her jaw was set and she had a death grip on the steering wheel. "You okay?"

"Yes. Why wouldn't I be?"

"I don't know." Lucas paused. "You seem...upset."

"I'm fine."

Silence stretched for a moment as he tried to figure out what was going on. It wasn't nothing. He suspected her reticence had something to do with the missing pieces of his life.

"Maybe this would be a good time for you to tell me what I've been doing since early February," he said.

Harper sighed and gestured to the glove box. "Open that up and grab the papers on top."

Lucas reached inside and removed the neatly folded sheets. "What is this?"

"One page for each month since February. I wasn't sure what the last thing you recall is, so I went back to a few days before we arrived in Fort Worth last February."

"I do remember Fort Worth. We pulled in on Sunday." He waved the papers. "This is a great place to start. Thank you."

"You're welcome. You hit close to forty events in the last six months. I didn't do nearly as many."

"Huh? Did I? I hope my bank account shows I'm in the black if I was that busy." His eyes rounded as he flipped the pages. "My placements are here too."

"I looked them up last night."

"You did? Wow. This is above and beyond." He glanced at her and then down at the paperwork again. "Thank you, Harp."

"You're welcome. I thought that if you remember the circuit, it might be easier to recall…other things."

"What 'other things'?"

Harper shrugged. "I was generalizing."

"What's this?" he asked, tapping the paper. "You even noted where we ate on the road?" Lucas laughed. "Apparently, you twisted my arm and got me to go to that horrible Tex-Mex place again?"

"It's not horrible." Her lips twitched. "They have the best chili relleno in three states."

Lucas chuckled. "So you say."

"You remember the restaurant. That's good."

"You're right. That is good. Too bad I don't recall eating there on this occasion." He looked at her. "What did I order?"

She laughed, and it was a soft, sweet melody. Ah, Harper's laugh. The sound buoyed him. She was always upbeat, even when he was fighting demons. "What you always order," she said.

"Fish tacos." They answered at the same time, and he laughed again.

Lucas examined the rest of the notations for February, pushing past the throbbing of his head. "Not bad. I took the number two spot, right behind Jasper Leonard. Respectable standings for an old guy."

"You're not an old guy," she said. "Look at each month— you can see how you're killing it."

"Aw, thanks. You've always been my biggest cheerleader." Gramps was right. He was blessed to have Harper in his life.

"Because you're one of the best saddle bronc riders out there, Luc."

Used to be, Lucas mentally corrected. He turned the pages slowly. "What happened in April?"

"I'm not sure what your schedule was since I was home much of the month. Gram had surgery."

"Surgery? What for?"

"She broke her hip. Trevor's wife, Hope, managed her home care for a while. She didn't bounce back like your grandfather did after his hip surgery," Harper continued.

"Her hip. Seems there's a lot of that going around." Gramps had hip replacement surgery over a year ago as well. "How's she doing?"

"We lost her, Luc."

Lucas snapped to attention, his heart hammering. "Bettie is gone?" He'd had a soft spot in his heart for Harper's maternal grandmother. The woman had insisted that he call her

Bettie, and she'd always sent Harper off with home-baked treats for him.

He reached over and squeezed her hand on the steering wheel. "I'm so sorry. I'll miss Bettie. She was the best." He couldn't imagine losing his grandfather. Lucas stared at Harper. "Did I at least attend the funeral?"

"You did." Harper swallowed, her eyes glassy with unshed tears.

"I'm so sorry, Harp."

He'd gone to the funeral and couldn't even remember. How lousy was that?

Lucas stared silently at the papers in his lap. After the news about Bettie, his focus was shot. He stopped and closed his eyes for a moment. "I'm not doing too well with reading right now, but I appreciate you putting this together."

"No problem." She slipped on her sunglasses.

"Anything else important happen that I ought to know about?"

"I…um…" She turned her head for a quick second and then stared straight ahead, her lips a thin line.

Lucas stared at her profile. The mahogany-brown tresses, highlighted naturally with red, were pulled back into a low ponytail. It was difficult to see her dark moss-green eyes behind the opaque sunglasses perched on her nose.

Moments like this, he appreciated how beautiful she was. Inside and out. Then he'd have to remind himself that they were friends.

Just friends.

Girlfriends came and went. But friends were forever, and he wanted Harper in his life forever.

"Is that a no?" he asked when she didn't answer.

Harper nodded, her eyes firmly fixed on the road.

Goose bumps ran down his arms and his gut said something was up. Yep, they'd been friends long enough for him to recognize the signs of trouble brewing. All he had to do was wait it out.

Trouble was, he suspected it had something to do with his missing memories. The more he thought about what it could be, the more his head hurt.

Not good, Morgan.

Not good at all.

Chapter Three

"Harper Elizabeth Reilly is in the kitchen."

Harper turned from the stove to see her father enter the room. Tall, with a build like a wrestler and a mop of red hair graying at the temples, Colin Reilly was an intimidating sight unless you looked close enough to see the laughing green eyes.

As the youngest of the three Reilly daughters, Harper had a special relationship with her father. She'd always been daddy's little girl.

"Are you making your famous chicken casserole for lunch?" he asked.

"No. This is to take to the Lazy M."

He opened a cupboard and grabbed a glass. "How's Lucas?"

"Not much has changed. He saw the neurologist yesterday. You know how much energy Luc has. Being sidelined is challenging."

"Your mother and I are praying for him."

"Thanks, Dad. Where is Mom, anyhow?"

"In her studio."

"What's she working on?" Harper had learned as a child that the downside of having Maureen Reilly, prominent sculptress, as a mother was that she couldn't be disturbed during studio hours unless it involved broken bones or blood.

"Your mother is completing a piece commissioned by a bank in Tulsa."

"That's impressive."

"It is." He filled his glass with water and then turned from the sink. "How long will you be home?"

"It depends on Luc's recovery."

"Luc's recovery." Her father was silent for a moment. Then he cleared his throat. "Your dear mother warned me to keep my mouth closed. But you're my baby girl, and I can't stand by and let you get hurt."

"Dad, please," Harper groaned. "Not another lecture about waiting around for Luc. We're friends. That's all."

That was the truth. The bitter truth.

"Now, Harper, I like Lucas. You know that. I just don't understand why a smart gal like you has followed that boy around for over twenty years."

Here we go again.

Annoyed, she turned back to the stove and added salt and pepper to the pan of sizzling chicken with a tad bit of force. "I've only known him for fourteen years."

"Huh. It sure seems like twenty years."

"I'm four years younger than he is. We went to different colleges. When I was in grad school, he'd gotten his business degree and hit the circuit full-time. It's not like I've been his shadow all my life."

"You have a marketing degree, but you tossed that aside to race a horse around barrels and follow Lucas around the country."

"Luc and I have different schedules. I don't follow him around." Indignation rose again and she dared to meet her father's gaze head-on. "Besides, I've made a nice living thanks to the rodeo. Far more than I would have in a midlevel marketing position."

She didn't like to brag, but she'd managed to parlay barrel racing into some lucrative ventures. There'd been magazine interviews and, last year, she'd been part of an endorsement deal with a popular women's boot line.

"I'd expect nothing less." He saluted her with his glass. "You're a Reilly. I'm proud of your horsemanship skills. But I paid for all those private riding lessons because I thought it was a hobby. Not a career path."

"It's what I enjoy doing right now. Don't you want me to be happy?"

"Apples and oranges. Of course, I want you to be happy. But you've run out of excuses, Harper."

"Dad." She knew what was coming next. Her father was about to launch into how she'd evaded what her parents believed was her destiny.

"You're home, and we're about to have an opening in the marketing department. And it isn't a midlevel position. How's that for a coincidence?"

Harper took a deep breath. Her father was a self-made man who had built the Reilly Pecans empire from nothing, and he expected his children to participate in the family business and give back to the community, as he did.

"Dad, I'm home because Luc is hurt. No other reason."

"I appreciate your concern for Lucas's welfare, but your mother and I raised you to make decisions about your future based on what's right for you as an independent young woman."

She opened her mouth to protest and he held up a hand.

"I've been upfront about my expectations, and I've given you far more leeway than your sisters. But it's time."

Time. Well, that was all well and fine for her sisters, who were delighted at the doors Reilly Pecans had opened for them. Both were married and happily settled into corporate life. Her oldest sister, by ten years, Madeline, a senior vice president, managed the various value-added products divisions of Reilly Pecans. Dana, five years Harper's senior, was another vice president. Of what, Harper couldn't recall.

The corporate office for Reilly Pecans was a five-minute drive from Maddy's home and Dana's condo in Oklahoma

City. OK City would be an hour-and-forty-minute drive for Harper from Homestead Pass. She'd be forced to move if she took the job. That meant finding a place to board her horse too.

Retiring from the rodeo circuit was definitely on her radar. But going directly from a saddle to a desk chair was not part of her plan.

Harper grimaced. "You want me to sit in an office in Oklahoma City and market pecans."

Her father pulled out a kitchen chair and sat down at the table. "I want you to market your family business."

Pecans. Harper couldn't escape them.

"And you don't have to sit in an office all day," her father continued. "Plenty of my employees are hybrid. I'm hybrid. You'd know that if you paid attention."

She looked at her father. "Dad, I—"

He raised a palm. "Pecans have been good to you, Harper. They bought this house. The biggest house in Homestead Pass. Pecans fed our family. Paid for college, your horses, and those lessons. We're more than blessed because of those orchards." Her father offered a sad smile. "There was a time when you were proud of the business."

"I am proud." Harper lifted the lid on a pan on the back burner and stirred the cream sauce. "Do we have to discuss this now?"

"Take a guess how many résumés have already come in for the position I want you to fill."

Apparently, they did have to have this discussion now. She gave a slow shake of her head as her father kept talking.

"Over fifty, Harper. Fifty on the rumor that I'll have an opening when one of our employees goes on maternity leave in November."

"How long would this arrangement be?"

He took a long drink of water and then met her gaze. "Six months. Just like your sisters. We'll start you as an intern learning from the ground up. Then ease you into the marketing position."

"Six months!" She blinked. "That's through February. Next year." Harper envisioned the life being sucked from her.

"Didn't you just say you were sticking around for Lucas? This seems like the perfect time to fulfill your obligation to your family." He narrowed his eyes. "Unless you have other plans."

Harper hesitated.

"As a matter of fact, I'm exploring several options," she said.

That was the truth. She'd heard through the circuit grapevine that she had been shortlisted for a big endorsement deal. Nothing concrete yet. Then there was the training school. Working with Luc, training riders, was her real passion. But that option was on hold until the bank approved the loan, and she could talk to Luc about the plans already in motion. Plans he didn't recall and might not be so happy about the second time around.

"Be that as it may, I want you to give the family business a shot. That was our arrangement."

"An arrangement made when I was a kid."

"You were eighteen and headed to college, as I recall. You understood the expectations. I'm asking no more of you than I did your sisters. Give the business a chance. If it isn't a good fit, you're free to step away."

"Are you saying that if I do a stint with Reilly Pecans and decide to go back to the circuit or any other career path, I'd have your blessing?"

"Absolutely." He offered a tender smile that reminded her that despite their differences of opinion, she loved her father dearly.

"I look at you, Harper, and I see potential. You can do anything. *Anything.*"

When he paused, Harper realized he was about to deliver the final blow.

"Maybe if you came to work for the company, you'd meet someone besides cowboys."

There it was. Arrow to the heart. Complete disapproval of the man she cared for.

Wounded, Harper turned to the stove. She added the browned chicken to a casserole dish before carefully pouring the sauce over the pieces. Silence stretched as she opened the oven and slid the baking dish inside.

"You hate the business that much?" her father asked quietly. Sadness laced his voice.

"Not at all. I haven't missed a harvest since I was six years old. That's the part of the business I enjoy. Not management."

"We can always find a place for you driving a tractor."

Harper chuckled and looked at him. "I don't doubt that."

"Your mother and I love you and want only the best for you." He paused. "This is an opportunity to secure your future."

His phone rang, saving her from responding. He glanced at his cell and cocked his head toward the hall. "I have to take this. Then we can finish this conversation."

Harper swallowed past the lump in her throat. The pragmatist in her whispered that her father had made some valid points. There was no escaping the fact that she wasn't getting any younger. Her days on the circuit were numbered. And now? Now, Lucas didn't recall that they'd created a plan for their future. Harper worked to push away the despair. Didn't the Lord have a hand on her?

She shook her head, refusing to allow circumstances to get her down. Her thoughts went to the flood story her father had once told her. There was a man sitting on a roof as the floodwaters rose. A boat and a helicopter came by to save him, but the man dismissed them as he waited on God. The man drowned and found himself standing before the Lord. It was the Lord who had sent the boat and the helicopter.

Maybe she ought to at least check out the position with Reilly Pecans. She didn't want to find herself with zero options. Even as the thought crossed her mind, a part of her cringed at the idea of even a day not spent out in the sunshine.

Minutes later, her father stepped back into the kitchen with expectation on his face. "Where were we?"

"Marketing Reilly Pecans."

"And your answer?"

"Two months. I'll know by the time your marketing person leaves what I want to do. And I'll only commit if I have the flexibility I'll need if Luc needs my assistance with medical appointments."

Two months was plenty of time to fulfill her obligation to give Reilly Pecans a chance, and hopefully enough time to bring Luc up to date on the training center plans without pushing him to remember.

Her father arched a brow, clearly surprised. "I'll consider your offer if you go into this with a smile on your face instead of acting like there's a noose around your neck."

Harper chuckled. "You have a deal."

The conversation with her father echoed as Harper drove to the Lazy M Ranch. This was not how she'd expected the last quarter of the year to unfold. She and Lucas were back to square one, thanks to his accident, and pecans were about to unseat her dreams.

Luc was part of those dreams, and it pained her to realize that everything she wanted had been within reach and was now very uncertain.

She'd met Luc Morgan when she was a senior in high school, and he'd come to talk to the graduating class at Homestead Pass High School.

His speech had been about going after your passion in life. Harper had taken his words to heart, knowing that despite the trajectory her parents planned for her, what she really wanted was a career in professional rodeo. She'd dared to approach him after the talk and ask for pointers on following that dream.

He'd encouraged her to complete college, as he had, and to sign up for events in her spare time. Sage advice that she'd followed.

That had started her segue to the circuit and her infatuation with the tall, charming cowboy. With Luc's career guidance, she'd entered competitions on the weekends and during college breaks. And they'd become friends. Good friends.

She shook her head.

Good friends.

The words weren't nearly as satisfying as they used to be.

Harper pulled up to the Morgan ranch house. She juggled the casserole in one hand and a gift bag in the other and pressed the doorbell. After minutes, there was no response.

Her soft knock on the door was promptly answered by Bess Lowder, the Morgan family cook and housekeeper. The woman was responsible for managing the Lazy M household since Luc's parents' passing. Dressed in her usual denim shirt and rolled-up blue jeans uniform, Bess held open the screen door.

"You don't need to knock, sweetie. You're just like family. Come on in."

Harper glanced in the living room as they moved down the hall in the direction of the kitchen. She stopped and did a double take. Every single surface was filled with plants and flowers. There were artful arrangements, freshly cut flowers, plants with big bows, even containers of succulents. The almost sickly scent of flowers overwhelmed Harper. She coughed and stepped away from the room. "What happened?"

"Oh that. All for Lucas. In the words of Gus Morgan, 'this place has been busier than a twofer sale at the Green Apple Grocery.'" She chuckled. "Smells like a flower shop as well."

"It does," Harper said.

Bess took the casserole from Harper's hands and dipped her head toward the kitchen. "I'll show you what else they brought." She opened the refrigerator door and Harper nearly gasped. Every inch was stuffed with casserole dishes and covered bowls. Glass and plastic storage containers lined the normally clutter-free countertop. Each had a label on top.

Taking a step closer to the counter, Harper read one of the labels. "Claire Talmadge? He dated her in college. I thought she was in New York City."

"Claire had her mother drop that off with a note that promised she'd be in town soon to see Lucas." Bess practically rolled her eyes.

The Homestead Pass grapevine whispered that Claire had asked Lucas to marry her the night of college graduation. Harper had never actually verified the validity of that story. Now she wondered, and her stomach knotted at the thought. She and Luc didn't cross the line to discuss personal relationships after a few missteps in the past.

More and more, Harper was beginning to think she had imagined the shift in her relationship with Luc.

Humiliation raced over Harper. "Who else?" she asked.

"Oh, honey, I have a list." Bess wedged Harper's casserole into the fridge and then turned to the counter. She opened a drawer and pulled out a legal pad. "I had to start documenting everything so that I can return the containers to the right gals."

"Gals? All this is from Luc's female friends?" Stunned, Harper took the legal pad and skimmed the list before placing it on the counter.

Bess nodded. "Former girlfriends, except for Ben at the barber shop."

Harper glanced around. "Where is Luc?"

"It's been a nonstop parade here since sunrise, which I suspect is due to Gus initiating the Homestead Pass chatter line yesterday."

"Is Luc okay?"

"Tired, is all. He's trying way too hard to figure out what happened between now and last February."

"But the doctor warned him about that."

"Yes. Gus told me about the doc's admonition." Bess clucked her tongue. "I called Trevor's wife, and she came by, checked his vital signs and did a quick neurological exam. She prescribed disconnecting the doorbell followed by a nap. That went over as well as you can imagine."

"Uh-oh."

"Yes. There may have been bribing with the promise of cinnamon rolls."

"Oh, Bess. I'm so sorry. I should have called first."

Bess gave a shake of her head, setting the gray curls in. "Nonsense. I told you. You're family." She smiled and ran a hand through her gray curls. "Gus says you're coming to Sunday dinner, right?"

"I hate to impose."

"I'm not here on Sundays, so it's not an imposition." She chuckled. "Olivia usually cooks." Sam's wife was a local chef and Luc had often raved about her cooking. "But not this week. There's too much food in this house that needs to be eaten."

"Good point." Harper held up the small bag in her hand. "I'll leave this for Lucas. It's that black licorice he likes so much. I stopped at the Hitching Post yesterday and picked up their last two packages."

"You are the sweetest."

A sharp knock at the front door had them both turning.

"More company. I'd better get that."

Harper scanned the kitchen counter when Bess left. A sinking feeling began in the pit of her stomach.

Once again, she questioned whether she had read the situation between herself and Luc all wrong. She thought what she'd seen in his eyes had meant there was something special between them. Now she wasn't certain of anything.

Harper eyed the names on the list again. Twenty women. She had zero intention of becoming number twenty-one on this list.

It occurred to her that her father was right about one thing. She knew better than to pin her dreams on a man. It was time to take back the reins to her future and fight for what she'd worked so hard for.

"Five thousand dollars!" Lucas put a hand to his aching head. "Are you sure? Maybe we should call the bank."

"Easy there," Sam said. "You're not supposed to get excited. As for the bank, it's after five p.m. The bank is closed."

Closed. Right. He should have remembered that.

After all his visitors yesterday, followed by mandatory napping, Lucas was ready to get on with his life, however limited it might be. An hour ago, he'd sat down behind the computer in the office at the Lazy M Ranch's main house to review his checking and savings account and realized the computer screen was only making his head throb and his vision blur. When he'd called Sam, who held the distinction of being a part-time accountant, his brother had come right over.

"What did I do with five grand?" Lucas paced back and forth across the hardwood floor of the office.

"I'm sure there's a simple answer. We'll laugh once we figure it out."

"Sam, you just reviewed my bank records. I withdrew five thousand bucks and I don't know why. I am not laughing."

"I'll lend you money if you need it. Now relax."

"Thanks, but I don't want your money and that doesn't help me figure out what happened." He rubbed his temple. "Why didn't I use my credit card?"

"Maybe you didn't want to max it out. Don't you use the credit card on the road?"

"Fair conclusion," Lucas agreed.

"It's showing as a withdrawal, but you didn't write a check. My guess is that you paid for something with a cashier's check." Sam continued to stare at the bank statement on the screen. "The only way to track that is to call the issuing bank. We can't do that until Monday."

Lucas dropped into one of the wingback chairs in the office. "What did I buy with five thousand bucks?"

"You've been talking about getting a trailer with living quarters."

"A trailer." Lucas perked up. "You're right. I have been talking about a trailer for a long time, so maybe I put a down payment on one." He scowled. "So where's the trailer?"

Sam shrugged. "Could be in Lawton. Harper would know."

"Okay, so if we go with that scenario, where's my copy of the cashier's check?" Lucas cocked his head and looked at his brother.

"Have you checked your wallet?"

He pulled out his worn, brown-leather wallet and examined all the folds and crevices. "Nothing but a receipt for burgers."

"What about the Wranglers you wore to the hospital?" Sam asked.

"I threw them in the washing machine when I got home, after I showered." He knit his brows together thinking. "Then I put them in the dryer. Haven't seen them since."

"I saw Bess folding towels when I came in," Sam said.

"Bess!" Lucas called. He scrambled out the door and down the stairs, with Sam thundering right behind him. At the bottom of the stairs, Lucas nearly collided with the housekeeper. He put a hand on her arm to steady them both.

"Slow down! Those stairs aren't a rodeo chute," Bess warned. "And you're supposed to be resting."

"Have you seen my laundry?" Lucas asked.

The housekeeper eyed him with a chuckle. "This is a laundry emergency?"

"Yes, ma'am," he said. "In a manner of speaking,"

"I couldn't dry the towels with your clothes in the dryer, so I pulled them out. Goodness, that was three days ago. They're still in a basket on top of the washer, waiting for you."

Bess did more than her job description spelled out, but she wisely never set foot in Lucas's room. Said no matter what she did, his room looked like a tornado hit the place the next day.

She wasn't wrong.

"Don't suppose you found anything unusual in the dryer?" Sam asked.

"Stuff that was in my pocket," Lucas added.

"Stuff in your pocket has been a given with your laundry since you were fourteen years old, Lucas." Bess smiled fondly. "There's a twenty-dollar bill, some change and a receipt that got washed." She pointed to the laundry room.

"A receipt!" Lucas pressed a kiss to her cheek. "I love you, Bess."

She eyed him suspiciously. "It's laundry."

"Today it's an answer to prayer," Sam said.

Racing into the laundry room, Lucas grabbed the basket and then headed for the kitchen. Hopefully, they'd solve the mystery of the missing money.

When he put the laundry on the kitchen table, Sam plucked the twenty off the pile while Lucas grabbed the folded piece of paper.

"You took my money."

"My accounting fee," Sam said. "Now, easy with that paper. Watch what you're doing. Maybe you should use tweezers."

"Have you got tweezers?" Lucas pulled open the kitchen drawers one after another, rattling utensils, before he closed each drawer quickly. "Nothing."

Sam leaned close. "Just be careful."

Lucas slowly unfolded the rectangle until it was in two pieces. "What's that say?"

"It's your portion of the cashier's check, all right. The ink's pretty faded, but it looks like it says Keller's Family Jeweler in Lawton, Oklahoma."

"Keller's Family Jeweler." Lucas could barely get the words out.

"Bingo," Sam said. "Looks to me like you bought jewelry."

"Where's the jewelry, and the box, and the paperwork that usually comes with a five-thousand-dollar piece of bling?" Lucas pulled out a chair and sat, his head spinning. "Sam, do you think it's a ring? Like an engagement ring?"

Nah, that couldn't be right. He would remember something like that.

He stared at his brother. "Could I have really asked someone to marry me?"

"Far-fetched as it may sound, I can't think of another plausible conclusion," Sam said. "Looks like you fell in love, little brother."

Lucas released a whoosh of air as reality hit like a punch to the gut. "Somewhere out there is a woman who has that ring, and I don't have a clue who she might be."

"Surely, Harper will know. Ask her."

"No way. That's not the kind of humiliation a fella goes looking for. Besides, Harper and I have a strict policy about mixing personal stuff into our friendship. I crossed the line once and almost ruined everything."

"What do you mean?"

"A couple of years ago, she dated some yahoo bull rider. They broke up and I let her cry on my shoulder and told her what I thought of him." He grimaced. "Big mistake. The next week, they patched things up, and she was mad at me for bad-mouthing him. She didn't speak to me for a month."

"That's not enough reason not to talk to her about this."

"Oh, there's more. I asked Harper's advice when I dated the Pawnee rodeo queen last year. Out of the blue, she blew up and kicked me out of her trailer. Told me if I couldn't see that the woman was only interested in changing her name to Mrs. Lucas Morgan then I was too dumb for her to be friends with." He whistled. "That was something else. Nope. I care too much about our friendship to risk alienating her with talk about another woman again."

"Fair enough," Sam returned. He glanced at the containers on the counter, turning to examine the labels. Then his brows shot up. "That's a lot of containers. From a lot of women. For the record, how many women have you dated?"

"I can't do that math. If you recall, I have retrograde amnesia. I can't remember the last six months."

"Ballpark then." Sam opened the fridge, pulled out a Dr Pepper, and flipped the tab. "How many exes can you remember?" He took a long swig from the can and eyed Lucas.

"In Homestead Pass or all together?"

"Seriously?"

"I'm a popular guy. Is that a crime?"

"Maybe." Sam counted containers. "More than five?"

Lucas raised his thumb to indicate more.

"Ten?" Sam jerked back as he said the word.

"More like a couple of dozen." He shrugged without apology. "I'm friends with all my exes. Doesn't that count?"

"You're going to have to reach out to them and see what you can find out."

"Aw, no. That will be downright embarrassing." Lucas stared at the receipt, his stomach twisting.

"Not as humiliating as it will be when your fiancée catches up with you."

"I guess I could call a couple of buddies first. If I can locate their numbers."

"Did Harper find your phone?"

"Dead."

"You know that you can pull data from a dead phone. Right?"

"No, I can't. It's an old model with a SIM card. A damaged SIM card."

"What is it? A flip phone?"

"No. Not a flip phone, wise guy."

"Well, you have the number for the jeweler. Call them on Monday and see if you can get any information. Maybe your fiancée picked out the ring."

"Brilliant." Lucas nodded and then grimaced. He had to stop shaking his head. "This receipt is for last Saturday. I must have gone to the jeweler before the accident."

"Yep. Last Saturday in Lawton. I think you'd better find a way to ask Harper without her catching on. She knows more than you think."

"*Harper?* Wait a minute." Lucas jumped up. "Harper dropped off my saddle and clothes." He raced out of the office and up the stairs, with Sam following. "Maybe the paperwork is in my duffel."

"Slow down. You're supposed to take it easy."

"You don't walk when the house is on fire," Lucas called over his shoulder. He grabbed the duffel and turned it upside down on the bed.

His clothes fell out, followed by a leather binder.

Sam grabbed the binder. "What's this?"

"Paperwork and schedules. Stuff I need on the road."

His shaving kit plopped onto the bed, followed by a black beribboned shopping bag that landed right on top of the duffel.

"Whoa. What's that fancy bag?" Sam asked.

Lucas snatched the bag and peeked inside. His jaw sagged at the sight of a jeweler's ring box. Hands shaking, he sank to the bed and pulled out the small black-velvet box. He stared at it for a full minute, unable to open the thing.

Sam grabbed the box from his hand and flipped open the lid to reveal a sparkling engagement ring. His brother whistled long and low. "I believe they call this a marquise diamond."

"Do they?" Lucas squeaked out the question.

"How did you manage to fall in love and buy a ring without telling your family?"

Lucas leveled him with a glare. "If I knew the answer to that question, or any of the two dozen you've asked since you showed up, I wouldn't be in this predicament."

"I'm going to go over your credit card transactions. Maybe you sent flowers or something, and I can figure out who you're courting."

"Flowers. I never thought of that." He paused. "Sam, you're not going to tell anyone about this, are you?"

"Who would believe me?"

"Good point. If this gets out, I'll be the laughingstock of Homestead Pass." Lucas frowned. "Gramps can never find out."

"You're getting a little paranoid, aren't you?"

"You know what Gramps calls me? The ice cream man. Says I have a new flavor each month."

"He isn't wrong. Though I sure don't know how you manage it." Sam looked him up and down. "You need a shave and a haircut."

Lucas ran a hand over his two-day growth. Wasn't any point in being a bronc rider if he had to shave every day. "Says who?"

"Everyone." Sam chuckled. "Although maybe we should rethink that. Apparently, there's a woman out there who wants to be your wife just the way you are. Or at least you think she does."

"So where is she?" Lucas asked. Where was his almost fiancée?

"I don't know. Out of the country? Or sitting home waiting for you to call."

"I guess that's possible." He let out a breath. "It's a relief to have found the ring. All I have to do is find the woman."

"Like that's going to be easy, given your history." Sam picked up the leather binder and unzipped it. "What's this?"

"I told you. Paperwork. Nothing special."

"Maybe there's information on your mystery woman in here." His brother flipped through the papers, a frown on his face. "Luc, this is a business plan for a rodeo training school. An extremely thorough and well-executed plan. The kind you show a bank loan officer." Sam shuffled through more papers. "Yep. That's what it is. And this is a copy of the bank loan application. All six pages worth. Signed by you and Harper."

Stunned, Lucas reached for the binder. "Let me see that." His gaze landed on the date the application had been signed. It matched the time they'd been in Homestead Pass for Trevor's wedding.

What was going on here? Why hadn't Harper said something on the way home from the neurologist? He'd asked if anything important had happened.

This seemed pretty important. He'd formed an official business partnership with his best friend and couldn't remember doing so. How did that happen? The plan had always been for him to go into business solo. He'd turned down her offer to collaborate numerous times and for good reason.

The training school was his opportunity to prove himself to his family.

"Good for you," Sam said. "You've talked about retiring next year. Guess I never thought you'd actually do the deed."

Head pounding, Lucas looked at his brother. "I have no idea where these papers came from."

"You don't remember this?" Sam asked.

Lucas put a hand to his throbbing head. "I remember think-

ing I ought to put a plan in motion for January. I sure don't recall doing it." Once again, things felt surreal, like he was living
someone else's life.

A buzz sounded and Lucas stood and pulled a cell from
his pocket.

"I thought your phone bit the dust," Sam said.

"This is Gramps's cell. I've ordered one online. Should be
here this week." Lucas stared at the text on the screen. "It's
Harper. She's checking to see what time she should be here
on Sunday."

"Sunday. Perfect. You can grill her then."

Lucas looked at his brother. "You're right. I need to figure
out what's going on with this business plan."

"Business plan? I want to know about the ring. The ring
that's missing a fiancée."

"Get real. I'm not going to mention the ring. Not yet."

Sam started laughing.

Lucas tucked the phone in his pocket and glared at Sam.
"What's so funny?"

"It just hit me that this is exactly like the prince searching
for his princess, getting women to try on glass slippers." His
brother grinned. "You know. *Cinderella.*"

"You're comparing my life to a fairy tale? That's not funny
at all."

"Come on, Luc. You hit your head, lost your memory, found
an engagement ring in your gym bag. You have no idea who
your intended is, and you're launching a business without your
knowledge." Sam nodded. "Oh yeah. It is kind of funny, and
it could only happen to you."

Lucas cringed at the words. His brother was right. It could
only happen to him. He'd lost his memory of the last six
months. A life where he'd made plans for the future that included settling down. Somehow he had to figure out exactly
what had happened.

Chapter Four

"**P**ass the brownies, Gramps." Lucas nodded at the plate in the middle of the kitchen table where he, Gramps and Harper still sat after his brothers and their families had departed only a short time ago.

"Not so fast." His grandfather held up a hand. "Those look mighty tasty, but they're deceiving."

"What do you mean?" Lucas cocked his head and assessed the square tin of frosted brownies.

"Son, no disrespect intended, but truth is, not all your girl-friends ought to be let loose in the kitchen." He looked at Harper, who snorted and then covered her mouth.

"They aren't my girlfriends," Lucas protested with a sharp glance at Harper. "And you can't mess up brownies."

"Ex-girlfriends then." The elder Morgan pushed the tin out of Lucas's reach and slid the plate of Bess's cinnamon rolls across the table. "Trust me on this."

Lucas examined the pastries and chose a plump roll thick with cream cheese frosting dripping down the sides over rib-bons of buttery cinnamon filling. The Lazy M Ranch house-keeper had a secret recipe for cinnamon rolls that brought grown men to their knees. That included him.

In turn, Lucas slid the plate to Harper. "Here you go."

"Seriously?" She held up a hand. "I'm still full from dinner."

"I'm never full," he returned. "And did I mention that your chicken casserole was delicious?"

That was an understatement. They'd reheated half the casseroles in the refrigerator for Sunday dinner and, hands down, Harper's was the favorite.

"He's right." Gramps offered an enthusiastic nod in Harper's direction. "Obviously, present company was excluded from my comment. You aren't one of his exes."

Lucas blinked at the comment. No, she wasn't. His glance moved to Harper once again. She seemed to be preoccupied with her coffee cup.

Why was it he and Harper had never dated? At first, it was because he was her mentor, and it wouldn't be right. Now, after years as close friends, he wouldn't do anything to risk that friendship. His girlfriends lasted a few weeks at most. Harper's friendship was for a lifetime. He couldn't imagine her not being in his life. Didn't want to even think about it.

"Nice to have a meal with the entire family." Lucas put on a smile and hoped his attempt to change the subject would work.

"Sure was." Gramps shook his head. "Woo-ee. Never thought the day would come I'd have so many great-grandchildren. Drew and Sam have two each. Trevor one." He looked at Lucas. "What are you waiting for? You aren't getting any younger."

Lucas jumped up. "Would you look at the time. Didn't you say you had to call Jane, Gramps?"

His grandfather checked his watch and stood. "You're right. We best get those dishes done before Bess finds them in the morning. Olivia started the dishwasher already, so we'll have to do these by hand."

"Harper and I can handle the dishes," Lucas said.

"Harper's our guest," his grandfather protested.

"It's only a couple of mugs and dessert plates. We got it. Besides, Harp and I have a few things to discuss."

"Okay. You twisted my arm," Gramps said. "I'll excuse myself then. Jane and I have book club meeting details to finalize."

"Who's Jane?" Harper asked when his grandfather had left the room. She picked up dessert plates from the table and moved to the sink.

"Jane Smith. Retired librarian. Remember her from Homestead Pass Middle School? She manages Sam's woodcraft showroom."

"Mrs. Smith. Yes. I do remember her. She and Gus are dating?"

"I thought so, but Gramps flat-out denies any such thing. Says they've been friends for years. He claims men and women can be friends without romance." Lucas raised a brow. "I suppose so. Look at us."

"Right," Harper murmured. "Look at us."

He turned at the undertone in her response. Had he imagined it? Harper didn't play games. Generally, she was an open book. So why did he sense red flags left and right of late?

They had lots to discuss tonight, but a part of him cautioned to take it slow. Something was definitely going on with Harper.

Familiar with the Morgan kitchen, she filled the sink with a squirt of dishwashing liquid and water and began to wash the dessert plates. Her attention remained focused out the large kitchen window overlooking the front porch and gravel drive.

Lucas finished off the rest of his cinnamon roll, picked up his plate and brought it to the counter. He grabbed a towel and plucked a mug from the dish drainer. "Everything okay in your world?"

"Me?" A musing smile touched Harper's lips. She looked at him. "You're the one with a shiner and a two-inch dent on your forehead. How are you?"

"A little better every day. My ribs are healing. Doesn't hurt as much when I laugh. I'm functioning on the hope that one day—" he snapped his fingers "—all my memories will be restored."

"It's only been a week, Luc. The doctor specifically said you weren't supposed to push yourself to retrieve your memories."

"But we can talk, right?"

"Talk? Is that what you were referring to when you told Gus we have something to discuss?"

Lucas opened a cupboard and put several mugs away. "How long are you staying in Homestead Pass? You're headed to Pasadena, right?" He clucked his tongue. "I'm sorry to miss that one. They've got a nice purse."

She eyed him. "You didn't answer my question. What did you want to discuss?"

"I'll get there. This is the scenic route." He looked at her. "Cali next?"

"No. Right now, it looks like I'll be Homestead Pass for a bit."

"Why?" Contemplating her answer, Lucas dried a dish, adding it to the stack before he turned back to her. "You're not hanging around because of me, are you?"

"Yes and no." She cocked her head to meet his gaze.

"What's that mean?"

"It means that's why I'm here now. You're my friend, and I won't leave if your health is compromised."

"I appreciate that, but I don't want to stand in the way of your career."

"You aren't."

"We can agree to disagree on that point." Lucas picked up another plate from the drainer. "You said yes *and* no. What's the no?"

Her hand skimmed the water, and she pulled out two forks. "I'm interning at Reilly Pecans starting tomorrow."

"Whoa! What?" The plate he held clattered onto the counter.

"Careful, Luc."

"Interning? Mind explaining that bombshell?"

Harper sighed and pushed her sweeping bangs away from her face with the back of her hand. "It's a Reilly rite of passage that I've been able to dodge for nine years. I may have mentioned it to you."

"I never thought you were serious about that."

"My father is very serious about Reilly Pecans." Harper sighed. "Traditionally, it's expected after college. Since I was busy with grad school and the rodeo, I dodged the bullet. Until now."

"I don't get it. Why intern?" Lucas asked.

"Because my father read me the riot act." She blew out a breath. "The plan has always been for me and my sisters to intern, fall in love with the business, and never leave." She shrugged. "You know. Happily ever after. The end."

"You agreed to this?"

"Agreed? If only it were that simple." She gave a small chuckle. "My sisters complied long ago. I don't have much choice. I'm home, and my father took the opportunity to remind me of my obligation."

"This is my fault," he said. "You're home because of me."

Harper waved a hand. "Not at all. This was inevitable. Besides, it could be worse. I talked him down from six months to two."

"What about competing?"

"On hold for now. I told you, I'm inching toward retirement."

"Give me a break," he groaned. "You're only thirty-two. You're not eligible for the senior category yet. The current two-time barrel racing champ is thirty-nine, and she's setting arena records left and right."

"Absolutely true." Harper looked at him and then away as pink touched her cheeks. "But maybe I'm getting a little tired of living out of a trailer after almost ten years of nomadic life."

He raised a brow. "Your trailer is nicer than most folks' homes."

"It's still a trailer. The thing is… I'd like to get married and start a family soon." She peeked up at him and then quickly looked away. "I'm trying to stay positive about all this. Who knows, maybe this will be a growth opportunity."

Lucas doubted that. What Harper liked was being in control and she thrived in wide-open spaces. Just like him. He was silent for minutes, thinking.

Marriage and kids.

Sure, of course. He couldn't expect things to stay the same forever. Didn't he want that too? A partner in life? Someone to fill the void in his heart? Wasn't that why he had an engagement ring in his duffel bag?

Harper deserved the best, and if that's what she wanted, he prayed the Good Lord brought her just that. Yeah, and he'd have to repeat that a few dozen times before his chest stopped aching at the thought of them going their separate ways someday after so many years as close friends.

She shot him a wary look. "Are you going to tell me what you wanted to talk about?"

"Ah, yeah. Um…" He cleared his throat. "I discovered that we've launched plans to go into business together. Going into business is a huge deal. Why didn't you tell me?"

She released the plug from the sink and dried her hands on a towel as the water and suds circled the drain with a sucking sound. "I suspected you didn't remember, and in truth, I dreaded having to convince you a second time."

"Convince me a second time? That sounds like we've had this conversation before."

Harper opened her mouth and closed it as though she had something to say but was holding back.

Lucas nodded at the table. "Let's sit down and talk. Okay?"

The chair legs squeaked as they moved on the oak floor.

Harper sat and folded her hands on the table. There was silence between them, the only sound the hum of the refrigerator.

He looked into her eyes, searching for an answer. "I really want to understand."

Harper lowered her gaze, concentrating on her hands before finally looking at him. "If you recall, you gave me 'the speech' in the truck when I took you to your doctor's appointment."

"The speech?"

"Yes. The one about how you have to do this yourself."

"Now you make me sound pigheaded."

She arched her brows. "You started talking about the training center two years ago. I asked to partner with you, and you flat shut me out."

"I do recall a few discussions, but I wouldn't say I shut you out."

"Please, all I've ever heard is how this is *your* project."

He looked at her. "You're telling me that at some point, I agreed to partner up with you."

Harper offered a solemn nod, her eyes on the table.

He'd been clear from the get-go that this was his venture. A project he'd kept to himself for a long time. It was an opportunity to build something that said Lucas Morgan wasn't just a pretty face with a brass buckle.

Sure, he'd made a go of the rodeo, but he wasn't a star, like Harper was.

Besides, this was the chance to step out of the shadows of his talented brothers. Though he was a fraternal twin, he'd always been the baby of the family. The baby who had to be protected because he'd worn his feelings on his sleeve when their parents died. Now, at six foot three, standing as tall as his big brother Drew, he still felt that he didn't measure up.

"Luc, I know how hard this is for you—not only are you injured, but you lost your memory. Grasping to remember details to fill in the blanks has to be the worst nightmare. But for a moment, think about how it affects those around you. It's a domino situation, and we're all struggling to understand what this means for the future."

Yeah, Harper was right. He was thinking. Thinking about the woman out there who might be expecting a ring.

"Luc? You okay?" Harper asked quietly.

Lucas rubbed his chin, still trying to understand.

"So that's why you've mentioned January several times." She nodded.

"Why would I change my mind about taking on a partner?" He knew he was being a jerk, yet he seemed unable to keep his mouth shut.

Harper straightened her shoulders, breathed deeply, and looked at him straight on. "Oh, I don't know, Luc. Maybe because we're friends, and you can't do everything yourself." Irritation laced her voice and her green eyes sparked with anger. "Clearly, you found the business plan. Did you read it in its entirety?"

Lucas swallowed. "No. Reading triggers headaches. Headaches start the whole cycle of dizziness and nausea."

"I'm sorry." She paused. "But if you had read it, you'd have realized that it's a good business plan. An impressive plan. I put in hours of research on that paperwork."

"I have no doubt that you did. Thank you." He ran a hand over his chin. "Look, I'm sorry, Harp. It's just there are so many puzzle pieces missing."

She nodded again. This time, her face reflected misery. Then she released a slow breath and looked away.

Well, he felt miserable too. It hadn't been his intention to hurt her.

"Where do we go from here?" he asked.

"That's up to you, Luc. The first loan application was rejected."

"Rejected?"

"Yes. You knew about the rejection. I took the liberty of tweaking the application paperwork and submitting it again. They advised me it might take longer to receive a response because the department manager was on medical leave. I'll check on things this week."

"What happens if it's approved?"

"You tell me." She gave a slight shrug.

He frowned. "I must have had a good reason to go against everything I laid out in my head for years. Too bad I can't figure out what it is."

Harper slowly turned her head and looked at him, her jaw sagging. "Excuse me?"

"That didn't come out as I'd intended."

"What did you intend?"

"I intended to express my confusion, and I'm trying to understand." He scrambled to move past his awkward and harsh comment. "If the loan is approved, how do you suggest we proceed?"

"We hadn't planned to start until January, but with you out of commission and both of us in Homestead Pass, we could begin now. Slowly. You're still in recovery mode and I have an obligation to my father."

We. We. We. How had things gone from a solo act to a team project? And how would he figure it out without alienating Harper?

"So, what does getting started look like?" His head began to ache from thinking, working to capture any scrap of a memory that would explain how this happened.

"We can discuss moving forward with contractors, if we get a green light from the bank."

Lucas nodded, trying to find the upside in the information. "Starting now will put the project a good six months ahead of schedule. That's an advantage. If I start the project in January, I wouldn't be able to start construction until spring. And, with calving, late spring."

"I forgot about calving," Harper said.

"Yep. Absolutely another advantage to starting now." He paused. "What happens if the loan isn't approved?"

She looked at him. "I think you should focus your energy on what will happen when the loan is approved."

"You're so certain it will be?"

"Nothing is certain, but I'm confident I provided an excellent business plan outlining a path to success. It will be up to you to decide if you can proceed with the project as a team."

"I don't like you leaving the circuit. I can tell you that much." He looked at her. "You have records to break. Buckles to win."

"That's moot. I already promised my dad. I'm here for two months. Besides, I told you. I'm ready for a change too."

She was in the right place for change. There were so many changes going on right now, he could hardly focus on one before another jumped out at him. "Harp, what if we get this project launched, and I can't ride again? Ever."

"The plan isn't dependent on you, or me, for that matter. Your name, yes. But not necessarily you in a saddle."

"That doesn't make any sense."

"Sure it does. If you recall… Oops, sorry. You can't recall." She took a breath. "We expanded the scope of the business plan to allow us to bring in other specialty professionals during the quarterly training sessions."

"Quarterly?"

"Yes. That's what we decided…" She looked at him. "You know. Before."

Lucas nodded. It made sense. Too bad he couldn't remember deciding to make sense.

"When the facility is not in use, we're going to allow other instructors to rent the facilities for private lessons."

Lucas jerked back with surprise. "Who thought of that?

It's genius. We'll be making money outside of our scheduled training school. Passive income. I love it."

"Right?" A smile turned up the corners of her mouth. "And with an outside arena and an inside climate-controlled facility, we have functionality year-round and the potential for twice the revenue."

"Two arenas? How can we afford two when there's equipment to purchase, not to mention horses?"

"We start slowly. It's all in the paperwork."

"Okay. Give me some time to process everything and get through the paperwork."

"Of course. Take your time, but you ought to know that I'm not walking away from this project because you can't remember. My future is at stake here."

He met her solemn gaze and nodded. This wasn't what he'd planned, but the Lord had other ideas. And if he had to have a business partner, who better than his best friend?

"I'm sorry, Harper. The last thing I want is to hurt you. This whole memory thing is overwhelming. It's like there are two of me, and the guy previously running my life forgot to sync his calendar with me before he went on hiatus." He paused. "Then there's the headaches and the vision issues on top of that."

"Sure. I get that. I hope you know that I'm praying every day for you. So are my parents."

"Thank you."

She stood. "I better get going. Thanks for dinner."

"Don't forget your casserole dish." Lucas stood as well.

"Yes. Right. Casserole dish." She picked hers up from the assortment of pans and plates that had been emptied and washed. "You sure have a lot of female friends."

"I guess so." His gaze followed hers to the counter. "Haven't seen most of them in a while."

"No?"

"Correction. I don't think I have." He paused. "Do you know

something I don't?" Maybe Sam was right. Maybe Harper knew the woman he was going to ask to marry him.

"I don't know anything, and I do not want to know anything." Harper held up a hand and backed away, looking everywhere but at him.

"Just asking." Lucas shrugged. "And by the way, I've decided to throw a little barbecue to say thank you and get all these dishes back to the proper owners."

"That's an idea. All your exes in one place at the same time. Sounds like fun." She made a gagging sound.

A phone began to buzz and Harper pulled hers from the back pocket of her jeans. She glanced at it and frowned.

"Everything okay?"

"Something is up at home. Dana and her husband just showed up at my parents' house." She looked at him. "Want to stop by and say hello?"

"Yeah, hard pass. Your dad doesn't like me."

"That's not true."

He rolled his eyes. It was true. Colin Reilly didn't have anything positive to say about their friendship, especially after Harper had joined the rodeo circuit. He didn't believe Luc was good enough for his daughter, and he was right. Too bad the pecan baron hadn't figured out that Lucas wasn't in the running for his daughter's hand. They were friends. Only friends. A mantra that was starting to wear thin.

"You better get going," Lucas said.

For a moment, she stared at him, her lips a thin line. "When's your next neurology appointment?"

"Next week or the week after. I have it written down somewhere."

"I'll go with you."

"You can't do that. You have a day job now."

"My father still owns the company. I can slip out early."

"We'll see." Today's conversation made him realize how

much he relied on Harper. Was that a good thing? Especially in light of her declaration to move on and settle down. Whoever the fortunate fella was, he sure wouldn't want Lucas hanging around.

He grimaced at the thought of being a third-wheel around his best friend.

"Are you okay?" Harper asked.

"Yeah. Headache."

She nodded. "I'll see you at the Kids Day Event on Saturday?"

"Yep. I'm going to assist Bess in the snack tent. If I'm really fortunate, I'll be able to pass out juice boxes and carrot sticks."

"Oh, stop."

"You have a good day tomorrow on your first day in corporate America. Play nice with the other kids. Make good choices."

She laughed. "I always do."

Yeah, she always did, which was why he didn't want to be the one who kept her from achieving everything she deserved in life. And as it stood, he wasn't happy about their business arrangement. Wasn't sure if he could handle his project becoming their project.

What could he have been thinking? Didn't matter. For now, he'd let things ride and pray the arrangement the other Lucas Morgan had made wasn't the biggest mistake of his life.

And Harper's.

Harper bit into her apple and stared out the window of the Reilly Pecans' employee lunchroom. Rain pelted the glass, creating a blurry gray visual that matched her mood. She found herself replaying the conversation with Luc over and over in her head and becoming more annoyed each time.

She'd thought they were on a trajectory to a shared future in more ways than one. Now, not only had the relationship been kicked into the red dirt, but he had reluctantly let the partnership stand in an effort to protect the only thing that really mattered. Their friendship.

That wasn't what she wanted. She wanted to go into the venture on equal footing, with the assurance that they both brought skills and dedication to the table that would ensure the success of the project. The way the situation stood left her unsatisfied, and she didn't like it at all, especially since she'd put so much into the training center plans. This project was her baby too.

She hadn't expected such a strong reaction from Luc about the partnership. Now she dreaded what would happen when he found out about the collateral attached to the second loan application. The one she'd planned to tell him about over dinner in Lawton the night of the accident. After their first loan application had been rejected by the bank, she had submitted the second application using land she'd inherited as collateral.

Harper held the title to a prime piece of property outside Elk City that she'd inherited from her grandmother. It was an option guaranteed to secure the loan without asking either Reilly Pecans or the Lazy M Ranch to back the venture. She had a spreadsheet all prepared to illustrate how they'd pay off the loan and remove the lien in their first few years.

Harper shook her head. Old Luc would've understood the rationale and have agreed in a heartbeat. New Luc would surely object. The last thing she wanted was to stress him and worsen his condition.

She hated being in this position.

Fortunately, she'd been going nonstop since morning, leaving her little time to mull over yesterday or to even think about the fact that new Luc didn't remember that they were at the precipice of a relationship before his accident. At least, she'd thought so.

Harper had gotten up at dawn to give her horse a workout, then showered and driven to the city.

Her new job kept her busy with paperwork and introductions. Everyone she met had been pleasant and welcoming. Of course, she was the boss's daughter, so they had to be nice. Harper had run into that dynamic often. As she nodded and smiled, it occurred to her that some of the employees she met were no doubt hiding resentment that as a nepotism baby, she was first in line for a coveted marketing position that others had worked years to qualify for. She couldn't blame them for being unhappy.

"Why aren't you eating in the executive dining room?" Her sister Dana slid into the chair across from Harper.

Harper shrugged. "You want me and my peanut butter and jelly sandwich and apple to eat in the executive dining room?"

"The chef in the executive dining room prepared turkey tetrazzini with porcini mushrooms. You could have eaten your pitiful lunch another day."

"Does Maddy eat in the executive dining room too?" Harper asked.

"Yes, though not today. She's working from home. One of her kids has a bug."

Harper nodded. "So where's Allen?" Dana's husband, a Reilly corporate attorney, had been by her side last evening when they'd announced the decision to celebrate their anniversary with a party at the Reilly mansion.

Dana sighed, her eyes overflowing with love. She held out her left hand and admired the diamond eternity ring on her finger. "He's in Tulsa for the day."

"That's quite the piece of jewelry." A beautiful ring, not unlike her sister's extravagant engagement ring. Harper knew when the time came, she'd opt for something simple.

"I'm so happy, Harp." Dana grinned, her eyes glowing. "I can't wait for our anniversary party."

Her sister's words brought Harper out of her musings. Looking at Dana was like looking at a petite version of herself. They both had the same wavy red-brown hair and green eyes. Dana, however, took after the maternal side of the family and was tiny and dainty.

Harper, at five foot eight, was all Reilly. She used to mourn her height, longing to be tiny instead of towering over boys in high school. Now she embraced her long legs and ability to reach the top shelf of the grocery store.

"I'm glad you're happy. But why do you need another party?" Only five years ago, the gardens of their parents' classic stone Colonial mansion had been transformed into an intimate wedding venue for two hundred. Harper's left eye twitched as she thought about the event and what she considered a waste of money.

"Oh, Harper, you wouldn't understand. Gathering our friends and family together for our anniversary allows us an opportunity to declare our love."

Harper bit back a snarky remark. Wasn't the eternity ring on her sister's finger a screaming declaration of their love? Dana was right. She didn't get it. To her, love was in the small unsaid things. It was actions, not words or diamonds.

And it was possible that Harper couldn't see things from Dana's point of view because she found herself a bit envious of her sister. Declaration of love. She sighed. Right now, all she could declare was that Luc was her best friend.

"I already spoke with Mom," Dana continued. "She's going to hire Moretti Catering."

Loretta Moretti. That was the first positive thing she'd heard since Dana had sat down. Sam's wife, Olivia, and her aunt Loretta were both phenomenal chefs. Harper would follow Moretti Catering anywhere.

Dana pulled out her phone and slid her finger across the

screen. "Allen is out of town for most of September, so I'm thinking this Saturday. Loretta has an availability."

"This Saturday? Isn't that kind of short notice?" Harper shook her head. "That won't work for me."

"Oh, come on. This is Homestead Pass, population ten thousand. What pressing engagement could you possibly have?"

"Don't bad-mouth your hometown. Homestead Pass made Reilly Pecans. And, as it happens, I have a charity event over at the Lazy M."

Dana sighed. "You can't get out of it? For your sister's party?"

"I won't leave them short-handed. I honor my commitments."

"Honestly, you're just like Daddy."

"I'll take that as a compliment." Harper smiled and tucked her apple core in her lunch bag.

"The only other date that works for everyone is three weeks from now. Tell me you aren't folding bandages for the Red Cross then."

"Very funny. I'll make the other date work." Harper paused. "How does Allen feel about a party?"

Dana shrugged. "Whatever makes me happy."

How different Dana's husband was from Luc. He'd never want to be obligated to the boss. Was he prideful or merely determined to be self-made? Probably both, though the latter sounded like her father. Maybe her dad and Luc had more in common than either of them realized.

"Is that your phone buzzing?" Dana asked.

Harper reached into her purse. "Yes. It's Luc. I better see what he wants."

"Lucas Morgan. The love-'em-and-leave-'em cowboy." Dana shook her head. "I spent quite a few of my college weekends at the rodeo trying to get his attention. He never noticed."

"You did? Really?" The words gave her pause. Luc and Dana? Her sister was much too high maintenance and Luc far too low maintenance. Was it wrong that she was pleased that Luc hadn't asked her sister out?

Dana laughed. "Yes, really. Oh, and I'm inviting Allen's cousin to the party. Also an attorney. He has potential. I'll introduce you."

"No. I do not want to be set up."

"You'll thank me later."

Oh, I doubt it.

Dana stood. She glanced at the industrial clock on the wall. "Benefits meeting in fifteen minutes. See you there."

"Yes, ma'am."

Harper dialed Luc's number and he answered immediately. "Luc, did you need something?"

"I left a voice message. You weren't supposed to call me back. I didn't want to interrupt your first day at work."

"I'm on lunch break."

"Oh." He released a breath, his voice hesitant. "I got a letter from the bank."

Her heart began to trot. "Open it." She'd rather find out now if it was bad news and move on to plan B. Not that she had a plan B.

"No. I'll wait until you can come by."

She swallowed, more nervous than she expected. "Okay, I'll be there as soon as I can."

"Take your time. I'm not going anywhere. I'll save you some dinner. Bess is making macaroni and cheese from scratch."

"My favorite. See you then."

Harper stood and cleaned up the table, tossing her lunch bag in the trash as she headed to the conference room. She had to give her father credit. The corporate headquarters was state-of-the-art, with every convenience at the disposal of the staff. If she hadn't grown accustomed to fresh air, the scent of horse and hay, and the dirt of a training arena, she might think this environment had merit.

Life would be a lot simpler if Reilly Pecans was her destiny. When Harper was six, her mother had signed her up for ballet lessons, as she had when her sisters had been the same age. Harper had hated ballet. She'd begged for horse riding lessons. Those lessons had set her on the road to meeting Luc. After that, she'd always thought horses and Luc would always be her future.

Was she wrong?

Chapter Five

Lucas did a double take when Harper left her truck and approached the steps of the Morgan ranch house. His boots hit the ground to stop the movement of the rocking chair. He stood to greet her, doing his best not to stare at the woman before him, tall and regal in a gray suit with a white silk blouse, her hair pinned to the back of her head.

"Harper Reilly. Is that you? Can't say I've ever seen you looking like the boss before." *Or looking so good. Period.* He tamped back that remark and focused on a potted begonia instead of her long legs.

She walked up the steps, her heels tapping on the cement, and then stopped to swat at a fly. "What are you talking about? You've seen me in a skirt plenty of times."

"This is different. You've gone all corporate."

"Oh, stop giving me a hard time. I'm cranky from fighting traffic, and I'm starving. Feed me, or I'll get a burger at the diner."

"Yes, ma'am." He held open the door, allowing the cool air to welcome them into the house and out of the humidity.

"Has Bess already gone home for the day?" Harper asked.

"Yeah, but I told her you were stopping by, so she made chocolate-chip cookies."

"I love that woman. I'm surprised someone hasn't stolen her away from the Lazy M."

"Don't even whisper such a thing." Lucas pulled out a kitchen chair. "Sit down and relax."

"Let me wash my hands first." Harper kicked off her shoes and put her suit jacket on the back of the chair before moving to the oversize farmhouse porcelain sink. "I'm not sure I can handle dressing up every day for work." She scrunched up her face. "And the commute. Ugh."

"Not much you can do about it, right?" He put a serving bowl of macaroni and cheese in the microwave and set the timer.

"I'll have work-from-home options after this week." She sighed. "If I make it that long. I didn't appreciate how blessed I was to have a career in wide-open spaces until now." Harper glanced at the counter and pursed her lips. "The stack of containers to return to your girlfriends is taking over the kitchen."

"Yeah, Bess said the same thing. And they're *ex-girlfriends*. I don't know why no one can remember that part."

"Potato. Potahto."

"The point is, I'm going to take care of the situation."

"And how will you do that?" She turned on the water and sluiced the liquid over her hands before reaching for the soap dispenser.

"I told you. A barbecue party. I'm thinking next Saturday. Got any plans?"

"Me?" She eyed him. "Why would I want to come to a barbecue featuring your ex-girlfriends?"

"For moral support. That's what friends do."

Harper's eyes rounded and she smiled. "Oh, is that what they do? Well, then have I got a deal for you."

He cocked his head. "What kind of deal?"

"Dana and Allen are celebrating their fifth anniversary in late September."

"Not sure I get the connection but tell them congrats from me."

"Or you could tell them yourself. My parents are hosting

an intimate party. If you agree to attend as moral support, in return, I'll come to your party."

Lucas grimaced and let out a loud groan. "That is not a fair deal. We're talking jeans and barbecue versus church clothes and unidentifiable stuff on water crackers." He shook his head. "Nope. Nope. Nope."

Harper shrugged and reached for a dish towel. "It's not un-identifiable stuff. Olivia's aunt is catering."

"She's catering my event too," he returned.

"Is she making cannoli? My sister specifically requested cannoli."

"No. We're having hand pies. She said cannoli doesn't go with shredded pork and ribs."

"Oh well. Maybe next time."

He couldn't help but smile. Loretta Moretti's cannoli. That sure changed the equation. A fella could put up with a lot for homemade cannoli.

"What is it you need me to do at this soiree?" he asked.

"Keep me from falling asleep. Create a diversion when my family tries to set me up with anyone they deem a suitable match. You know, the usual."

For a long minute, Lucas debated, finally capitulating when he thought about the cannoli again. "Fine. I'll do it."

"Wonderful." Harper smiled sweetly and then turned to the microwave without missing a beat. "Oh, that smells lovely."

Clever gal. Move on quickly so he can't change his mind. She knew him too well.

Harper glanced at the plate and silverware already on the table. "How can I help?"

"I got this," he said. "Bess made cornbread muffins too. Don't suppose those might be of interest?"

"Absolutely. I earned them today."

"Was your first day at the office that bad?"

"Not bad, simply not what I'm accustomed to. Actually,

the morning zipped by. It was the afternoon that was terminal." She walked to the table and sat down. "I was with two other new hires. We sat through hours of presentations. At one point, my legs started twitching from sitting still so long."

The microwave beeped and Harper shot up from the chair. "I'll get that."

"Harp, I got it." Lucas grabbed potholders from the counter.

"You've never waited on me before. No sense starting now."

"Sit," Lucas said. "You're tired, and you're my guest." He carefully removed the serving bowl, bubbling with buttery cheesy noodles, and placed it on a trivet in the center of the table. "Want a rundown of my day?"

She eyed him cautiously and unfolded the cloth napkin on her lap. "Do tell me about your day, Lucas."

"I organized and filled goodie bags for the Kids Day Event. Stickers. Pens and pencils, notebooks, and little Bibles. I filled more than one hundred bags. Then I stocked the prize booth."

"Prize booth?"

"Yeah. The kids get tokens when they arrive, and they can earn more at each activity. The tokens can be turned in at the booth for prizes." He pulled plates from the cupboard as he spoke and placed them on the table.

"What a great idea. Who thought of that?"

Lucas bowed as he put a tin of golden-brown cornbread muffins and a tub of butter on the table. "Me. I saw something similar at kid's rodeo up in Montana and told Trevor about it."

"That's really genius." She glanced around. "Do you have any honey?"

"Sure do," he said. "Do you want a salad with that meal?"

"No, thanks." She shook her head. "I prefer languishing in carbs."

Harper added a healthy amount of macaroni and cheese to her plate before slathering butter and honey on a muffin. Then she said, "Let's pray. Fast. I'm starving."

She took his hand. "Lord, thank You for Your abundant blessings, for our new ventures, and for patience. Lots of patience. Bless this food to my body. Amen."

"Amen," he murmured, slowly releasing her soft fingers.

She wasted no time digging in. Lucas had never seen a woman enjoy food like Harper. Despite her appetite, she never gained an ounce. His glance skimmed over her trim figure before he quickly looked away. *This is Harper*, he reminded himself. *No checking out your best friend.*

"Mmm. This is amazing." Harper held a spoonful in the air. "I need to get the recipe. We eat macaroni and cheese from a box at my house."

"You're joking, right? I thought you had a chef."

"We've had a few over the years. My father always fires them, and my mother is hopeless in the kitchen." She licked her lips and glanced around. "Don't tell her I said that. She's a fabulous sculptress and a wonderful wife and mother, but a terrible cook. Once, she lost track of time in the middle of a piece and nearly burned the kitchen up."

Lucas chuckled.

"Time…" Harper repeated. Her spoon clattered to her plate and she wiped her lips with the napkin. "I nearly forgot why I stopped by. Where's the envelope?"

Lucas stood and pulled a slightly wrinkled, thick white envelope from his back pocket.

Eyes round with excitement, Harper clasped her hands together tightly. "Come on. Open it, Luc."

"Okay," he said on a sigh. He wasn't nearly as excited as she was. No matter what the letter said, there were decisions to be made.

Lucas slid a finger under the flap. He tore open the envelope and pulled out the papers inside. The cover letter was short and to the point.

"'Dear Mr. Morgan and Ms. Reilly. I have good news. Homestead Pass Bank has approved your loan for the proposed training center.'" Lucas skimmed the other papers. "Looks like approval conditions and financing numbers."

Harper released a short gasp. "May I read it?"

"Sure. Your eyes are better than mine right now. I'm still getting headaches when I read." He handed her the letter, along with several other papers. For minutes, she intently read each page and then looked up at him.

"I'm thrilled, but I don't want to get ahead of myself, Luc. Have you been praying about this?" she asked. "Do you want to proceed?"

"Sure. Ah, yeah."

Harper dropped her head. "I don't want your grudging acceptance of a partnership, Luc."

"It's not grudging acceptance." No. That didn't describe what was going on in his head, because he couldn't even pinpoint those emotions. Once again, the guy he used to be had stolen how he was feeling now, leaving Lucas confused. The same question rattled around in his aching head. Why had he agreed to a partnership in the first place?

"Right. Hold back that enthusiasm, pal." She pushed her plate away and looked around. "I'll take those cookies now."

Lucas grabbed the plastic container from the counter and put it in front of Harper.

"What about you?" he asked.

"What do you mean?" Harper asked.

"How can you start a business when you have a full-time job?"

"A temporary full-time job," she said. "Besides, I'm good at juggling."

"Why do you want to do this, Harper?"

"Why?" Her gaze moved from the cookie to him and then away.

"Yeah. You have lots of options in the equine community,

not to mention Reilly Pecans can open any door you choose. Why a training center with a broke-down cowboy?"

"You are not a broke-down cowboy. And I already told you why. Retirement is in the not-too-distant future. I want to choose that future instead of having it decided for me." Harper tensed. "And I certainly do not want my father's name granting me opportunities I haven't earned."

She lifted her head and eyed him long and hard with hooded green eyes. "I've earned this opportunity, Lucas. And I believe that we can create a training center that will prove to be something we both can be proud of."

He raised his palms. "Easy there. I'm simply trying to figure out where we go from here."

"If you want to proceed, we should meet with an attorney who can help us file the appropriate documents."

"An attorney. Do you know any?"

"Naturally, Reilly Pecans has quite a few on retainer, but I'd rather not involve my father."

He looked at her. "Have you mentioned any of this to Colin?"

"Not yet. I will eventually. I'd rather tell my father after the internship is completed. I promised him I'd give Reilly Pecans a chance. I don't want to hurt his feelings. He's convinced I'll fall in love with the company." She looked at Lucas. "I'm sort of between a rock and a hard place."

Lucas ignored her murmured words. "He's not going to be happy that you and I are doing business together."

"My father is not complicated. He has a plan for Reilly Pecans. Anything that obstructs that plan makes him unhappy."

She was right. The wrath of Reilly was unavoidable. Her dad would no doubt blame Luc for keeping his baby girl from her true destiny.

"How about you?" she asked. "Have you spoken to your family?"

"No family discussion, if that's what you mean." He raised

a hand. "Sam stumbled on the business plan in my binder. Any reason why I can't tell the rest of the family?"

"No, of course not. We agreed not to involve family in the financing, that's all."

"Sam's a certified public accountant. What if he recommends someone he's worked with?"

"That'll be fine with me."

"What about registering a name?" Luc asked. "Got any ideas?"

"Luc you already chose a name. Homestead Pass Training Center." She looked at him. "You know. Before your accident."

"Huh. Well, glad I'm doing something besides losing my memory." He looked at her. "So no Morgan and Reilly in the name? We decided on that?"

"If we put Reilly on there, someone is bound to think it's something to do with pecans. We didn't want to confuse anyone with Morgan Ranch or Reilly Pecan references."

"Wish I could recall that conversation. I might be a tad more enthused about things if I could." He rubbed his head.

"I'm sorry," Harper said. "I feel bad that every time we discuss this your head aches and you look stressed. That's exactly what the doctor said to avoid."

"Don't apologize. None of this is your fault." Lucas slid into a chair and worked to find something to say that might make them both feel better.

"Who died?" Gramps walked into the kitchen, his boots clomping on the wooden floor.

"No one died," Lucas said.

"Then why the long faces?" He moved across the room to the coffeepot, where he removed the carafe and examined the liquid, his face contorting with pain. "Who made this swill?"

"Bess did before she left," Lucas said.

"I suppose I'm forced to drink Dr Pepper." Gramps pulled

open the refrigerator, grabbed a can and approached the table. "What's going on?"

"Remember back when I talked to the family about someday using my parcel for a training school?" Lucas asked.

"When you retire. Yeah, that's the same as when pigs fly, right?" His grandfather took an empty chair.

"No. I'd been thinking of retiring in January. With this injury, the timeline has been moved up."

Gramps popped the lid on his soda. "That's great news."

"That's not quite all the news," Harper said. "Luc and I are going into business together."

"Oh." Gramps frowned.

"What do you mean? What does 'oh' mean?" Lucas asked, anxiety rising.

"Many a friendship has been torn asunder because of a business deal, son."

"'Torn asunder'? Did you make that up?" Lucas asked.

"No. That's pure Gus Morgan."

"Mom and Dad started Lazy M Ranch together, and it was a very successful venture. What about that?"

"Aw, that's different," Gramps said. He took a long swig of soda. "Your momma and poppa were married. Committed."

"We're committed." He looked at Harper, searching her wide green eyes. "Aren't we committed to this plan?"

"I am. I don't know about you." She opened the plastic container once more and reached for another cookie.

"I'm committed," he said a little too loudly.

"Well, there you go," Gramps said. "You're both committed. Sounds like your dreams are going to come true."

Lucas slid his glance to Harper once again. She looked at him and then focused on the cookie in her hand, but in the brief moment they connected, he'd seen confusion in her eyes. Maybe because she'd seen the fear in his.

Sam's wife, Olivia, had once told him that the best dreams

should scare us. Starting his own business was a dream come true. A business with Harper, however, terrified him. What if he failed and took her with him? What would happen to their friendship?

He couldn't let that happen. He wouldn't.

Show me what to do here, Lord. Show me Your will for this situation.

Gravel crunched and the smell of diesel filled the air as the second of three yellow school buses, rented for the Kids Day Event, rumbled toward the Lazy M Ranch exit. Harper chuckled as she waved to the elementary-aged children on the last bus. In return, they smooshed their little faces against the glass and waved back, laughing and giggling.

"This was a good day. It was so much fun helping those kiddos ride the donkeys." She pushed her bangs back from her slick and sweaty forehead and turned to Luc. "Eighty degrees of heat and humidity that only August in Oklahoma can offer, and yet a perfect day." She sniffed the air. "Except that I now smell like donkey."

Luc pushed his straw Stetson back and leaned close. "Aw, not too bad."

"It was worth it. I haven't had that much fun since I helped out with Sunday school class when I was in high school. Today reminded me how much I enjoy working with children." She looked around the grounds, where white tent peaks dotted the landscape. The bright-colored Kids Day banners that had been stretched between the tents moved back and forth in the breeze.

"Trevor has quite the ministry with this event," Luc said. "This is the third year, and they doubled the number of kids bused in from Oklahoma City. Pastor McGuinness is tickled at the success."

"That's fantastic."

"It is. My brother is making a difference in the community. In the world." He paused. "I want to do that."

His response had Harper's mind whirling. "You know, the training center will be open well before next summer. I'm sure we can find a way for our training center to be part of the next Kids Day. I'd like that. Wouldn't you?"

"What do you have in mind?" Luc asked.

"A small rodeo might be an option. Mutton busting and roping. I'd be up for a barrel racing demo."

"Hmm."

That was all he said as half a dozen more ideas popped into her head, but she held back. She recognized that her enthusiasm could be a lot to handle. Blame it on the Reilly genes. The old Luc had understood that and it had never bothered him. The new Luc's expression said that he needed more processing time.

She missed the old Luc.

"Care to check out the training center property?" he asked Harper.

"Sure." They'd already checked out the property a dozen times when they'd been home for the wedding, but Luc didn't remember that. She'd take his interest today as a good sign. Maybe being in the space would trigger his memories.

"Hey, you two."

Harper turned to see Trevor, Luc's fraternal twin, approach. His adopted young son, Cole, trailed behind with an energetic brown-and-white border-collie-mix pup.

The cowboy certainly had changed in the last year. She would have labeled Trevor solemn and circumspect in the past. No longer. A smile lit up his face, and love shone in his eyes when he turned and nodded at something Cole said.

Yes, that's what falling in love did to a guy.

A mere two weeks ago, she thought she'd seen something in

Luc's eyes. She shot him a quick sidelong glance and sighed, more confused than ever.

"Thanks for your hard work today," Trevor said as he stepped closer.

Luc grinned. "We had fun, Trev."

"Ditto that," Harper added. "Now, how can we help with cleanup?"

"Oh no. You've done plenty," Trevor said. "Cole here has a whole cleanup team ready."

"Way to go, Cole," Luc said with a grin. He offered the shy thirteen-year-old a high five. "I knew I liked you for a reason."

"Thanks, Uncle Luc," Cole mumbled.

"Who has the keys to the UTV?" Lucas continued. "I want to take a ride over to my parcel with Harper."

Trevor pulled a jangling ring of keys from his back pocket and tossed them to Harper, who caught them easily. "Here you go. Don't let him in the driver's seat."

"Nope. I won't," she said with a wink.

"Well, you're no fun," Luc said.

"And proud of it." Trevor smiled at Harper. "Good to see you, Harper. Are you coming to the battle of the exes?"

"Battle of the exes?" Harper snorted and burst out laughing. "Oh yes. I'll be there. I'm bringing popcorn and a lawn chair."

"Oh, go on, you two," Luc grumbled. "It's a barbecue party. A polite gesture to thank my friends for their kindness when I was down, that's all."

Trevor's lips twitched. "Anyone else notice that the guest list is all women?"

"Not true," Luc protested. "The ranch wranglers, including Slim Jim, will be there. Ben from the barbershop is coming as well."

"Ah, Ben. Cole and I were there last month." He ran a hand over Cole's summer buzz cut. "You know he cuts hair, right?"

Luc pulled off his straw Stetson and pushed back his waves

of brown hair. "I have that on my to-do list. I clean up real nice. Don't I, Harper?"

She stepped back. "I am not incriminating myself." Nor would she admit that she liked Luc's disreputable brown shaggy hair as is.

Trevor laughed as he pulled a cell out of his pocket and read the screen. "That's Hope. She saved us cupcakes." He looked at Harper and Luc as he looped an arm around Cole's shoulders. "See you two later."

Harper turned to see Gus Morgan heading in their direction, his boots kicking up dust as he strode across the compact red dirt.

"There you are," Gus called. "I've been looking for you." He gave Harper a nod of greeting as he approached.

"Me or Harper?" Luc asked.

"Lucas Morgan is what the boxes say. There's at least ten of them, and they're filling up the kitchen."

"Boxes. What boxes?" Luc asked. "Where did they come from?"

"I surely don't know the answer to that question," Luc's grandfather returned. "Didn't look close enough."

"Do you want to go up to the house first?" Harper asked.

"Nah, it's probably ranch supplies accidentally sent to the house. Sometimes they put my name on them instead of Trevor's. I'll check it out later." He turned to his grandfather. "Thanks, Gramps."

"No problem. I'm heading to Jane's. She picked up my book club read from the library, and I'm anxious to get started. There's leftover meat loaf in the refrigerator." Gus laughed. "If you can get to the fridge."

"I'll get the boxes cleared out."

Harper matched her steps to Luc's as they strode to the equipment barn where a UTV waited for them outside the building.

"I've always wanted to drive one of these," Harper said. She examined the olive drab color of the doorless off-road vehicle.

"Don't you have one at the orchards?"

"Several. But only the staff are allowed to use them."

"No perks for being the boss's daughter?"

"Oh sure. Perks aplenty. All the pecans I can crack. Cinnamon-roasted pecans come autumn, and from the added-value division, there's pecan divinity at Christmas."

"I love Reilly pecan divinity," Luc said. "I'm also partial to the pecan praline." He smacked his lips.

"I remember," Harper said. It was tradition for her to bring pecan treats to the Morgan household every year between Thanksgiving and Christmas.

They slid into the side-by-side seats and fastened seat belts before she backed up the vehicle and headed across the pasture toward the gravel and dirt road that cut through the Lazy M. A billow of red dirt followed them once she maneuvered the UTV onto the road.

"Easy there," Luc said. "I'm feeling every last bump."

Harper let out a small gasp and lifted her boot from the gas. "Oh, so sorry. I forgot."

At the fork in the road, she slowed and turned left. Straight ahead was where Drew had built a house for his family at the top of the hill. Sam and Olivia's place was to the right and along the eastern pasture. This was pretty land covered with bleached summer grasses that extended to a rolling backdrop of fir trees.

They were headed to a paved private road that separated two halves of the property. Luc's parcel bordered the road. Minutes later, an aged one-story log cabin came into view. The notched horizontal logs had faded to a dull gray. A porch and railing surrounded the cabin, though the railing had fallen down in several spots.

If possible, the building seemed sketchier than the last time she'd been here, no doubt due to the summer storms of the last few weeks.

"Did you ever decide what you want to do with the cabin?"

"Was it under discussion?"

Harper shot a glance at Luc. "For some reason, a discussion came up at Trevor's wedding. Drew had mentioned razing the place, and you said you wanted to think it over."

"The cabin stays. I should have made that clear right away." He narrowed his gaze. "I don't know why I would have said that."

She parked the vehicle beneath the canopy of a huge oak tree and got out. Luc followed. He approached the cabin slowly, hands in his back pockets, and stopped and stared. "My dad took Trevor and me on great adventures in that cabin. It holds a lot of memories."

Luc normally spoke only in generalities about his parents. He'd never shared much about their death, and she hadn't pried, recognizing the Do Not Enter signs he'd erected when she'd ask a question or two. Yet, after all these years, she longed for him to let her in, if only to understand him better.

She sensed that today was different. Or maybe it was that Luc was different. "What kind of adventures?" she asked.

"Overnight camping trips. Just the three of us." A soft smile touched his mouth. "Taught us how to pitch a tent right there." He pointed to a grassy area to the left of the cabin. "One time, Trev and I were about ten years old, and we insisted on doing it all ourselves. I remember that night like it was yesterday. The mosquitos were biting, and the air was thick. We rushed to set up the tent and get inside..." His voice trailed off.

"Fun night?"

"Oh sure," Luc nodded. "We played Go Fish and board games until we fell asleep. There was a rude awakening when the tent collapsed in the middle of the night. While we scrambled around trying to figure out what to do about it, the skies opened up and the rain decided to teach us another lesson."

"What did your dad do?" Harper asked.

"Dad laughed." Luc smiled, his eyes glassy as he continued to stare at the cabin. "Said there was very little in life that wasn't worth laughing about." He cleared his throat and turned to her. "I seem to have forgotten that lesson."

Harper nodded slowly. Now she understood why he'd chosen this parcel. Because it reminded him of his father. Sure, there was pain associated with this land and the cabin, but there was joy in the memories as well.

"I have no doubt we can salvage the place," she finally said. "Make it part of the training school experience."

"Part of… I don't follow."

"The cabin. How about a merch store?"

"Merch?"

"Yes. Training center merchandise. You were the one who originally mentioned ordering merchandise. T-shirts, hats, saddle blankets. Then there's mugs and water bottles." She grinned. "Think about it, Luc. Visitors could purchase popcorn and soda and snacks at the cabin to take to arena performances."

"Merch, huh?" Luc cocked his head, confused. "Be nice if I could remember my brilliant ideas so I could take credit for them."

"Your memory will come back eventually." She started for the cabin. "Come on, let's take a look and see how much work it's going to need."

"Slow down there, Harp. Those steps aren't as trustworthy as they used to be."

Harper raced up the wooden steps before Luc's warning registered. A crack sounded and both of her booted feet dropped through the aged and splintering boards. Her balance off, Harper waved her arms, struggling to regain her stability before she face-planted forward.

She froze when strong hands circled her waist, both keeping her upright and startling her.

"Don't move," Luc commanded, his breath soft in her ear.

"Oh, that's not going to be a problem."

"Are you hurt?"

"No, my boots and jeans protected me." She worked to raise her legs. "What I am is stuck." Stuck and dazed from Luc's touch.

"Hang on. I'll get the tire iron from the UTV."

He returned a few minutes later and knelt next to the steps, pounding at the boards, randomly removing the rotted and dusty pieces one at a time. "Okay, yank your feet up."

Harper glanced at the boards scattered around her and then at the remains of what was once a railing. "I need something to hold on to."

"Right. Right." He examined the situation. "Put your arms around my neck and I'll haul you out."

She grimaced at the potential humiliation the solution held. "Couldn't you just give me your arm?"

"What? That won't work. Put your arms around my neck, would you?"

"Fine," Harper muttered. Though she turned her head as she slipped her arms around his neck, she couldn't help but inhale a combination of Luc's aftershave and a healthy dose of awkward embarrassment.

He pulled her free from the steps and whirled around, dropping her lightly on the ground. Harper stumbled away from him as though she'd been zapped by a cattle prod. Goodness, she'd never been that close to Luc in her entire life. His arms around her seemed foreign and somehow yet right. Too right.

Then she recalled that she wore eau de donkey perfume and looked like a hot mess. She nearly groaned aloud.

"Thanks," Harper said. Avoiding his gaze, she bent over to brush the dust and debris of the ancient wood planks from her jeans and inspect the material for splinters, praying he wouldn't notice the embarrassment burning her face.

"Are you sure you're not hurt?" he asked. Concern laced his voice.

"I'm fine. The porch isn't, but I am."

"Guess this place needs more work than I wanted to admit. I'll start repairing the cabin as soon as possible. The doc didn't tell me I couldn't do a little carpentry."

"Sam's a carpenter. Maybe he has time to help."

"Aw, I don't want to bother Sam. He's already helped me out a lot since I got back. He's plenty busy with his woodworking projects and obligations at the ranch."

Harper shook her head at Luc's stubbornness. "He's your brother," she finally said. "In fact, Drew probably has a thought or two about the cabin as well."

"That reminds me. What about the plans for the training center? I recall seeing the drawings in the business plan. Who did we hire?"

"A friend of Drew's, but he's had to pull out of the project due to a job move. We talked about hiring Drew."

"Good idea. I'll talk to him. Oh, and I meant to tell you that Sam's attorney friend can fit us in late Wednesday afternoon. His office is in Oklahoma City. Sam is going to drop me off for another appointment earlier in the day. Think I can hitch a ride home with you?"

"Sure, but what do you mean he's going to drop you off? Drop you off where?"

"I was referred to a neuro-optometrist in the city for evaluation." Lucas shrugged and gave a chuckle. "Maybe I'll need glasses. Think that will make me look smart?"

Harper turned her attention to Luc's face and took in the

two-day beard, the straight nose and his blue eyes the color of a calm summer sky. It was the face of a man you could count on.

Look away, she commanded herself.

"Luc, you are smart. You graduated from college with a business degree."

"If I was smart, my life wouldn't be upside down."

"Stop that. None of this has been in your control. Now tell me, what does a neuro-optometrist do?"

"They specialize in vision rehab from traumatic brain injuries. I'm not sure what he can offer me, but after over two weeks of living someone else's life, I'm ready to try anything."

"A specialist. That's encouraging."

"It is if I can start using the computer and reading without triggering a headache."

"That would be huge," she agreed. "So, you have an appointment and then you'll meet me at the attorney's office?"

"Yeah. That work for you?"

"Absolutely. Maybe we could have dinner afterward and discuss our progress."

"Good idea."

"Thanks, Harper." Luc gave the cabin a long look. "I'd really like it if we could make the cabin have a purpose in our plans."

"I don't see any reason why we can't make that happen."

Harper stared at the structure for a moment. It seemed that all of their steps of late were coming together to create something bigger than she and Luc had imagined when they'd started uniting their dreams. She could only pray that Luc saw that too. And perhaps it might help him to recall that they'd been on the path to uniting their hearts as well.

Chapter Six

Lucas reached for the door handle to exit the attorney's office at the same time Harper did. When their hands tangled, he stepped back. Quickly.

"I've got it." He placed his palm on the door, doing his best to avoid accidentally brushing against Harper as she moved past him onto the sidewalk.

Saturday's incident at the cabin continued to haunt him, the feel of Harper in his arms distracting him at odd moments.

This was Harper. His friend. The revelation that he was attracted to his buddy had startled Lucas to his core. More than that, it confused him. And he sure didn't need any more confusion in his life. So, yeah, he'd avoid the whole touching thing from here on out. Or at least until he figured out what was going on.

A car horn had him glancing at five-o'clock traffic backed up on the street. He was grateful they would have dinner before heading back to Homestead Pass. There was something to be said about living in a town where heavy traffic meant five cars waiting for the light at the intersection of Edison and Main.

"That went smoothly," Harper said.

"Hmm?" Lucas looked down at her.

"The attorney," Harper said. "Where were you?"

"I'm here. Lots on my mind." He nodded as her comment

registered. "Thanks to your meticulous planning and preparation, everything has gone smoothly."

"Not a big deal," she demurred. "I wasn't looking for a pat on the back."

But it was a big deal. Despite his memory loss regarding how they'd gotten to where they were right now, and his misgivings, one thing was obvious. Harper had all the chops of an astute businesswoman. Sure, he might toss in a few good ideas here and there, but Harper held the reins that directed the operation.

It's not that he'd thought Harper was just a pretty face. That wasn't it. Long ago, he'd realized she was smart as can be as well as the consummate athlete on the circuit. Over the last three weeks since the accident, he'd discovered that she was a lot like her father as well—a leader with a natural head for business.

"You're wrong, Harp. It is a big deal. The guy was impressed with how you had everything ready to go. Dotted all your i's and crossed your t's is what he said. You made us look like we know what we're doing." He paused. "I know I've given you a lot of grief, but old Lucas and new Lucas both agree that you're doing a bang-up job."

She cocked her head and smiled, her green eyes sparkling. "Was that a compliment?"

"Yes. Absolutely a compliment, and you know what? It occurs to me that you're a lot like your daddy."

Harper rolled her eyes and started walking down the long stretch of sidewalk, her heels clicking on the pavement. "I am not even going to ask what that means."

Lucas shrugged and matched his steps to hers, taking note once again of how different she looked. Today she was all corporate in a suit and heels. Different in a way that messed with his head.

"All I'm saying is that, despite my issues, I appreciate what you've accomplished."

"I'm starving," she returned, shutting down the topic. "Are you hungry?"

"Oh yeah. My stomach has been rumbling for an hour. Where are we eating?"

"How about Italian, since I never got my ravioli? There's a cute little place around the corner and a block over that looks promising. Somewhere between fancy and a dive joint. Dana says the tiramisu is almost as good as Olivia's bistro."

"I'm in," Lucas said.

Harper looked at him. "Do you mind walking since the weather is so agreeable?"

"Not at all. Lead the way."

The aroma of sweet basil, oregano and tomatoes teased Lucas mercilessly as they settled into a soft pleather booth with menus. A smiling server took their beverage orders and placed glasses of ice water dripping with condensation in front of them.

Lucas grabbed a crisp grissini from the basket in the middle of the table and perused the menu. Thankfully, the lighting in the place wasn't too subdued, and the font was legible. Reading had become increasingly challenging lately. His glance landed on ravioli, and he looked up at Harper. "What did you mean you never got your ravioli? Were you talking about Olivia's restaurant?"

"No." She leaned forward. "We arranged to meet for dinner the evening of your accident."

"Saturday? We did?"

"Yes. Milano's Italian Restaurant in Lawton."

"Milano's," he murmured. Sort of a fancy place as he recalled. Maybe celebrating?

She scanned his face as though searching for a sign that he

remembered. He didn't, though he sensed from her expression that this was a critical piece of information.

Lucas closed his eyes for a moment and could almost grasp the edge of a memory dancing on the periphery of his mind.

Milano's Italian Restaurant.

With Harper.

Almost. Then it was gone.

He looked at her and shook his head at the expectation in her eyes, which confirmed his gut intuition. There was something important about that dinner they were supposed to have. Lucas desperately longed to figure out what he couldn't remember.

"Sorry, Harp." Lucas released a long breath. "I have nothing."

"It's okay." She said the words softly.

"Is it? I feel like there's something off between you and me." He reached into his pants' pocket, pulled out two black pens with white script, and placed them on the table. "It would be real nice if I could recall stuff like ordering ten boxes of merchandise."

"The boxes? I take it they weren't farm supplies?"

"Nope."

Harper picked up a pen and rotated the barrel to read the print. "'Homestead Pass Training Center.'" She looked at him. "You ordered pens?"

"Oh, so much more than pens." Lucas began to count on his fingers. "There's also notepads, mugs, water bottles and ball caps." He shrugged. "I even got the name right."

"What? No T-shirts?" She gave a small laugh.

"Maybe they'll arrive next week. You were right. Apparently, I was very excited about this project when I placed the order."

Excited when I placed the order.

Lucas paused to mull his choice of words, sneaking a quick peek at Harper. She hadn't noticed. The date on the invoice was June. Yep, less than three months ago he'd been so enthusiastic about their joint business venture that he'd spent what amounted to a night's prize purse on swag.

Fast forward to now and he couldn't even recall how she'd become his partner. Once again, he was left feeling like he'd been dropped smack-dab into the middle of someone else's life.

"Seriously?' Harper chuckled. "Ten boxes? Where are they?"

"After Gramps tripped over them, I shoved them in the empty guest room."

"I like the colors you went with," she said. "We talked about colors and logos a few months ago."

"Did we talk about ordering pens?"

"No. But think positive. You now have merchandise for our cabin store." She took a sip of water. "How's that going? The cabin, I mean. Did you talk to Sam?"

"Ah, not yet." He studied the menu, hoping she'd let it slide.

"Not yet as in 'I can do it myself'?"

"Something like that." This time he met her gaze, silently pleading for her to let it go.

Harper opened her mouth and closed it as if she, too, wasn't looking to argue.

When their server interrupted with mugs of fresh steaming coffee and prepared to take their food order, Lucas made a mental note to leave a large tip.

"Butternut squash ravioli sounds good to me as well," Lucas said as he relinquished his menu.

He and Harper sipped coffee in silence for a moment. Good coffee. Lucas looked around. Nice place too. Not as nice as Moretti's Farm-to-Table Bistro, of course. He couldn't help but wonder about Milano's again. He and Harper usually favored hole-in-the-wall places on the road. Authentic and low-priced cuisine.

"Did I thank you for taking off work early to pick me up?" Lucas asked.

"You did. Twice." She set down her cup. "Tell me about your appointment with the neuro-optometrist," Harper said.

"Turns out I probably needed reading glasses all along, but the doc isn't going to prescribe them until I've had at least four weeks of visual rehab."

"Visual rehab? You mentioned that before. How does that work?"

"I'm about to find out. All I know is that they tossed a lot of information at me today. Doctor speak. Words like *neurological event*, *visual motor balance* and *optometric visual therapy* were thrown around. The gist of it is prism lenses and eye training exercises. Once I get started, I'll be able to do some of the exercises at home."

"That's good, right?"

"I sure hope so. The goal is to eliminate the headaches, dizziness and anxiety when I read."

"Anxiety?"

Lucas looked around and then leaned closer. "Yeah. I get pretty anxious when I start to read, and my vision doubles or the headaches start and I get nauseous. It's a hamster wheel I haven't figured out how to dodge."

"It must be frustrating. Did he offer anything promising regarding riding?"

"I'll progress to riding with a helmet at all times once the vision issue is under control. I can drive then as well." He paused, his eyes wandering to the wavy grain of the wood tabletop. "But I'll never be going back to the circuit. I know I'm retiring and all, but it's different when you walk away on your own terms as opposed to not being able to get back in the arena because someone else has put the nail in your coffin."

"I'm sorry, Luc." She reached out and touched his hand.

Lucas grimaced at the jolt. There it was again. His pulse

shot to Mach 3. He slid his hand away and studied his water glass.

"Thanks. I'm trying to focus on the positive. I'll be back in the saddle eventually, and I won't have to drive with Gramps." Lucas chuckled. "Have you ever driven with my grandfather?"

"I don't think so. I'm like you. I rarely relinquish my driver's seat."

"Well, let me tell you, it's like being on a tour bus. He stops to chat with everyone he knows. The man randomly signals, pulls over and rolls down the window. Yesterday, it took us an hour and a half to go from the ranch to the grocery store." Lucas shook his head. "By the way, Mary McAfee at the inn is having a bunionectomy next month. Her second. Winnie at the post office has a cousin whose son joined the army. And keep it under your hat, but Pastor McGuinness has a suspicious mole on his back."

Harper's laughter spilled out. "That's more news than I got from yesterday's *Homestead Pass Daily Journal.*"

"Right?"

"Harper Reilly? Is that you?"

Harper swiveled quickly in her seat, eyes rounding with surprise. "Dallas!" A grin split her face as she jumped from her seat and flung her arms around a tall cowboy. Slightly embarrassed, she stepped away a moment later and motioned toward Lucas.

"Luc, this is Dallas Pettersen." She turned to the cowboy. "Dallas, meet my good friend, Lucas Morgan."

Slowly unfolding himself, Lucas rose to his feet. He narrowed his gaze and gave the young cowboy a slow assessment. The kid could have modeled Western clothing for a magazine with his crisp short-sleeved checkered shirt, razor-creased Wrangler jeans and spotless white-straw Stetson. The glossy buckle at his waist had been polished bright enough to blind a person in the sunlight. His face was clean-shaven with no stubble to be seen, emphasizing the angles of his jawline.

Though annoyance had Lucas frowning, he offered the other man his hand. "Pleased to meet you."

"Lucas Morgan? In the flesh. Wow, I've been following your career since I was a kid. I consider it an honor to meet an old-timer like yourself. Why, you have more time in the saddle than I have on the earth."

Ouch. That hurt.

"That might be a slight exaggeration," Lucas muttered. Even if it were true, men had been challenged to a duel at noon for less in the old Western days. He cocked his head. "How is it you two know each other?"

Harper looked at Dallas and they both laughed. "I know his parents. Family friends. I babysat Dallas and his sister when I was in college." She smiled. "I remember many a night helping you with sixth-grade algebra."

Dallas grimaced. "Don't remind me."

Lucas did the math as he ran a hand over his two-day beard. Dallas was somewhere around twenty-one or twenty-two. No way Harper would be interested in a kid that young.

His glance went from Harper to Dallas as the two old friends grinned at each other.

Or would she?

And why did it matter to him? They didn't interfere in each other's romantic life. Yep. That rule had been established years ago, he reminded himself. Harper was looking to settle down. He ought to be happy.

I'm happy for her, he repeated over and over in his head.

Lucas unclenched his fists and eyed the other cowboy while working on his happy face.

"What are you up to these days, Dallas?" Harper asked. "I heard you graduated from OSU last year."

The kid nodded. "Yep. Took the LSATs in the spring and

sent off applications to law school. Now I'm hitting the circuit while I'm in wait mode."

"A cowboy lawyer. I love that." Harper turned to Lucas. "Very cool, right?"

"Oh yeah. Love it," Lucas returned. *Almost as good as a stick in the eye.*

"What about you? What are you doing in the city, Harper?" the cowboy asked.

"In town for business."

Dallas nodded, offering the full wattage of his smile. "Well, it's really good to see you."

"You too." Harper lifted a brow in Lucas's direction. "Would you like to join us for dinner, Dallas?"

Nope. Nope. Nope. Lucas willed the kid to refuse the offer.

"Oh no. I don't want to interrupt." Dallas nodded and gestured to the back of the room. "I've some buddies waiting for me. Wait until I tell them who I met." He shook his head slowly. "The two of you are like rodeo royalty."

"Not quite. But thanks for that, Dallas," Harper said with a laugh.

"Now, be sure to give me a call, Harper. I'd love to jaw about old times."

Right. Old times. Lucas glanced around. Where was that ravioli?

"I'll do that," Harper said and gave Dallas another hug.

"Nice to meet you, sir," the younger cowboy said.

"You, too, kid." Lucas sat down and gave a short laugh as the cowboy strode away. "Old-timer? Seriously?" he grumbled.

Harper slid into the booth. "Come on. We are getting old."

"Not me. I don't ever plan to get old. I'll be like Gramps. Frisky and sassy until the Good Lord takes me home."

"I don't doubt that." A soft smile touched Harper's lips. "Still, time keeps moving, pal. Though it seems like I was babysitting Dallas only yesterday."

"And now he's six foot tall and flirting with you."

"He was not." Eyes averted, Harper folded her napkin on her lap while her face turned pink.

Lucas laughed. "Yes, my friend. He was."

"Dallas is much too young for me."

Lucas glanced across the room where the young cowboy sat with his friends. After a minute, Dallas turned and met Lucas's stare.

"Too young for you, huh? Maybe you ought to tell him that."

The icy stare he leveled at the cowboy had the kid offering a quick nod before he turned back around. Yeah, the youngster was definitely crushing on his one-time babysitter. And Lucas wasn't quite sure why it annoyed him so much.

"There's a condo for sale in our community," Dana said.

Harper chased the last crumbs of mocha-chocolate birthday cake from her plate and then looked up at both of her sisters who sat across the family dining room table. It seemed she was always outnumbered at family events since Gram passed—Harper on one side of the table and her sisters and their spouses on the other.

"Did you have a nice birthday, Maddy?" Harper asked.

Her eldest sister chuckled at Harper's dodge of Dana's words. "I did. We left the kids with a sitter. Edgar and I had a lovely dinner at a new restaurant in the city before we came here for dessert."

Edgar nodded absently while he shot stealth glances at his smartwatch. Harper didn't quite understand what her sister saw in the tall, silent, tax attorney, but apparently there was someone for everyone.

"Hello. Did you hear me, Harper?" Dana persisted.

Harper smiled politely and reached for her water glass. "Were you speaking to me?" She tried not to sigh too loudly.

The trouble with being the youngest was that everyone seemed determined to run her life.

"Yes. I said there's a condo on the market in my community. It's five minutes from work. There's a wonderful workout facility in the member's center, and we're only steps from the golf course and the country club." Dana turned to Allen. "We love our place. Right, honey?"

Allen glanced up from his dessert plate, looking confused for a moment. "Right. Right."

"You and I could commute to work together when Allen is out of town," Dana continued.

"Dana, I agreed to a two-month internship. Let me take things one day at a time," Harper said. She had zero desire to move to the city.

"Your father and I are so excited that you're working at the company." Her mother tucked a lock of short blond hair behind an ear and beamed at her youngest daughter. "Have you made a decision about the full-time position?"

"Not really." Harper cut herself another small wedge of Maddy's birthday cake. This was her third piece. If the conversation didn't detour to someone else soon, she wouldn't fit into her jeans. "Who made the cake? It's yummy. The raspberry jam filling is sublime."

"Mom special ordered it from a new bakery in Elk City," Dana said. "I've ordered our anniversary cake from there."

Undeterred, Harper's mother waved a hand in the air. "Sweetheart, you're going to have to give me a little more than that. Are you at least enjoying yourself there?"

Harper blinked. She disliked being in this position. Her parents were so certain two months at Reilly Pecans would change her career path. "Well, um…the training program is comprehensive. At the end of the month, I'll start working with the gal who's leaving. As her assistant."

"That's wonderful. You wouldn't be placed in such an important position if you weren't smart and talented."

Or the boss's daughter. Harper bit her lip. She hated contradicting her mother, especially when she was the parent who asked so little of her.

"Maureen, I know our girl will to be a force in the company." Colin looked at his wife and then around the table, his expression tender. "Won't it be wonderful when all our girls are part of Reilly Pecans?"

Oh terrific. Now she was going to break her father's heart.

Harper searched for a topic to divert the direction of the current train wreck. "You'll never guess who I ran into this week." She grinned and glanced around the table. "Dallas Pettersen."

"Dallas?" Her mom smiled. "How is he?" She shook her head. "Now you've reminded me, I should reach out to his parents. It's been so long."

"What's Dallas up to?" Maddy asked.

"Prelaw," Harper said.

"Dallas was always a good kid," her father said. "You could do worse."

Harper's jaw sagged. "Dad, I am not dating Dallas."

"Why not?"

"Oh my goodness. He's at least ten years younger than me, and I thought you didn't like cowboys."

"Age is only a number," her father said. "And you mentioned prelaw. Another attorney in the family couldn't hurt."

"I am not dating Dallas." She shoved another bite of cake into her mouth, savoring the sickly-sweet buttercream.

"What's the story on the construction that's about to begin at Lazy M Ranch?"

"What?" Harper's head popped up and she stared across the table at the ill-timed comment from Maddy's husband.

Edgar, of all people. The man never spoke at family gatherings. Tonight he chose to break his vow of silence? Harper swallowed hard and prayed that no one could see how unnerved she was.

Eyes on her plate, she responded. "I, um… What construction?"

"A friend of mine is consulting on a project that's about to break ground out there this autumn. I'm certain he said the Homestead Pass Training Center on the Lazy M Ranch."

"Oh that." She gestured with a flip of her hand. "Lucas is retiring and launching a rodeo and equestrian training center."

Dana blinked and leaned forward, hands clasped, elbows on the table. "That's huge news, Harp. Why haven't you said anything?"

"What's to say?"

"What do you mean 'what's to say'?" Dana continued. "Normally, all we hear is Lucas this and Lucas that."

"You're right, Dana. You should talk to Lucas about the project." Harper eyed the exits and picked up her fork again.

"Did I understand correctly that you're half of this project?" *Edgar!*

Harper gripped the fork tightly. She glared at him. So much for sharing the news about the training center in her own time. Preferably, after the internship was completed.

"I'm more like a silent partner until my obligations with Reilly Pecans are met."

"How silent?" her father asked, his stare piercing.

"Maybe this isn't the place to discuss Harper's personal business," Maddy offered.

Harper glanced around the table. Despite Maddy's attempt to toss her a life preserver, all eyes remained on the youngest child.

"Harper, is all this true?" her mother asked.

"Ah… Yes."

"So this was the other option you were talking about?" her father asked.

"One of them. Yes. Financing has been up in the air. We only just received the green light from the bank."

Folding her linen napkin and placing it on the table, Harper worked to keep her voice level and calm. They couldn't see her hands shaking, could they?

"When did all this come about?" her mother asked.

"Oh, we've been kicking around the idea for some time." *That's right, Harper. Keep it casual.* "We both planned to retire in January. When Luc injured himself in August, the timeline was accelerated."

"You didn't tell your mother and I you were going to retire in January," her father said. "I would have remembered that."

Harper looked from her father to her mother. "I would have told you once all the details were ironed out."

"The details." He shook his head. "And how did you two finance such an undertaking, anyhow?"

Harper hesitated. "Dad, do we have to have financial discussion now?"

"I don't see why not. We're all family here." He glanced around. "We don't have secrets. Do we?"

Her eyes followed his, only to find everyone following the conversation with way too much interest.

"I used the property Gram left me as collateral," she finally said.

"Without discussing it with your mother or me?"

The dining room was silent, the tension uncomfortably thick and awkward.

"It's her inheritance, Colin," her mother interjected. "And she's thirty-two years old. You started Reilly Pecans at that age. I don't recall you asking anyone's permission. Don't you think we should be proud of her initiative?"

Relief flooded through Harper at the words. She mouthed a thank you to her ally as the odds shifted in her favor.

Colin released a sizeable harrumph. "I hope you feel the

same if she loses that inheritance, Maureen." He turned to Harper. "I'd like to see your business plan, young lady. And I'd like to know how your commitment to Reilly Pecans fits in with this project with Lucas."

A slow pounding started at Harper's temple. "I'm happy to have you review my business plan when I have the opportunity, Daddy. As for my commitment to the family business, it remains unchanged. I promised you two months, and I intend to keep my promise."

The answer failed to soften her father's expression.

"I can't believe you're leaving the circuit," Dana said.

"That's up in the air as well. I might still rodeo on the side." She cleared her throat. "As I said, retirement was on my radar for next year. The timeline for the school has been moved up with Luc's injury."

Edgar gestured with a hand as if ready to add to the conversation. Before he could, Maddy stood. "Not another word, Edgar." She glanced at her watch. "The babysitter is on a tight schedule. We're going to have to wrap this party up."

Dana stood, as well, and looked at everyone. "Don't forget. My anniversary party is coming up."

"How could we forget, Dana?" Maddy murmured. "You've reminded us a dozen times."

"Now, Madeline," Colin said. "Be nice. Your sister is very excited."

Harper's phone buzzed amid the intensifying white noise of family discussion. She stared at the device, grateful for the diversion.

It was Luc. Oh boy, could she use a dose of Lucas Morgan right now.

"I have to get this. It's very important." She pushed back her chair and dashed out of the room and out of the house to the front portico with its massive pillars.

She pressed the answer button. "Luc, what's up?"

"Am I interrupting anything?"

"Not a thing." The warm breath of evening embraced her as she spoke. Harper relaxed against a column, hidden from the tall windows of the dining room.

"Are you sure? You sound…funny."

"Just another night at the Reilly's. We celebrated Maddy's birthday. Edgar threw me under the bus. Oh, and my father is furious about my life choices, as usual."

"Why furious?"

"He found out about the training center and doubts my commitment to the pecan business."

"Furious sounds pretty serious."

"I don't want to talk about it." She paused. "What's up with you?"

"Did you show him the business plan? Colin will be impressed if you show him the paperwork."

"We didn't get that far. And I really do not want to talk about it." Further discussion would only stoke Luc's belief that her father didn't like him.

"Okay. Sure."

"You called because…"

"You didn't RSVP for the barbecue party tomorrow night."

Harper chuckled. "It's not like you sent out formal invitations or RSVP requests."

"No, but we made a deal, and I'm verifying that you're still coming, thus upholding your end of our bargain."

"Getting nervous?" she asked.

"You have no idea. I haven't had a party since Trev and I turned eight."

"That's not true. You told me that Gus threw you a graduation party after college. Mini golf in Oklahoma City."

"Not the same thing. Besides, I'm the host. I've never hosted an event before. It's a huge responsibility."

"Loretta Moretti is catering. There's nothing for you to do but smile and enjoy your guests."

"Easy for you to say."

"Absolutely. Because never in a zillion years would I throw a party for all my exes."

"How many exes do you have?"

"Not many, and yet I still wouldn't ever be so foolhardy." She paused. 'I'm not sure I understood your rationale for this event in the first place. A party to return dishes?"

"Think of it as a giant thank-you card. Besides, I'm fortunate to be alive, and I want to celebrate that."

"Gratefulness. Okay, I can get on board with that. Embrace it for the next twenty-four hours and you won't be nervous." Harper paused. "'In everything give thanks.'"

"Sounds familiar."

"First Thessalonians 5:18." A verse she ought to embrace as well. Life was all upside down right now. Despite how things appeared, the Lord never changed. That was what she should focus on.

"'In everything give thanks,'" he repeated. "I like it. Short and to the point." Luc paused. "Are you sure you don't want me to talk to Colin?"

"No. Absolutely not." Luc talking to her father could only add fuel to a simmering fire.

"Alright. If you say so." He was silent for a moment. "See you tomorrow, Harp."

"Yes. Thanks, Luc."

"Thanks? For what?"

A smile escaped as Harper imagined Luc's intent gaze upon her. His blue eyes concerned.

"Thanks for being my friend," she answered.

"Any time, buddy. Any time."

Harper slid the phone into her pocket and moved closer to the windows that framed the front of the house, revealing the dining room and hall. Maddy and Edgar stood in the foyer, saying their goodbyes, along with Dana and Allen.

She reached for the doorknob, praying the bell hadn't rung on round two of dinner with the Reillys.

"'In everything give thanks,'" she whispered.

Chapter Seven

Trevor poked his head into the kitchen. "Luc, there's a guy outside who wants to talk to you about a horse."

"Is that the start of a cheesy joke?" Lucas laughed, picked up his coffee mug from the kitchen table and took a long swallow.

"Nope. There's a guy outside with a mare. Says you bought her."

Lucas glanced at the wall clock. The barbecue party kicked off in less than an hour. "I knew it. Everything's been going so well up to now. Of course, the other boot had to drop."

"Howdy, Ms. Moretti," Trevor called.

Loretta Moretti turned from the counter where she and a catering assistant reviewed notes on a clipboard.

"Trevor, lovely to see you. Will all your family be with us tonight?"

Gramps stepped into the kitchen. "Yes, ma'am. The boys and their wives got babysitters so they could be here tonight to support Lucas."

"Wonderful," Loretta said. "I haven't seen your handsome grandsons all together since Trevor's wedding."

Trevor smiled and put a hand on his grandfather's shoulder, leaning close. "Are you sure they aren't here for the entertainment portion of the show, Gramps?"

"That too," Gus chuckled.

"Is there entertainment besides the band?" Loretta asked. "I wasn't aware."

"No," Lucas said. "That's just Gramps being facetious. No worries."

Loretta nodded. "What about these containers on the kitchen table? Could you remind me why they are here?"

"They belong to our guests and, hopefully, they'll claim them before the night ends," Lucas said.

"I see." She smiled and waved a hand at the stack of dishes on the counter. "Well, if you'll excuse me. There's some last-minute preparation to be done. Guests will be arriving any time now."

"Oh sure." Lucas nodded. "I gotta see a man about a horse."

He stepped outside with Trevor behind him to find a gray-haired cowboy, wearing a smile that lit up his leathery face, approach the house.

"Son, let me apologize for taking so long to get here. I tried to call you half a dozen times, but your voice mail was full, and I couldn't get through. I plain gave up. Good thing you drew me that map to your ranch."

"Thanks for coming out. When was it I bought the horse?"

The cowboy blinked at the question. "Early August."

Lucas nodded. "As it turns out, shortly after that, I hit a tree with my pickup and lost a good bit of my memory."

Pushing back the brim of his worn and yellowed straw cowboy hat, the older man cocked his head. "So you've got amnesia? Like in the movies." He clucked his tongue. "Well, ain't that something."

"Yes, sir. It surely is," Lucas agreed. Though "something" didn't even begin to cover the last few weeks.

"Are you trying to get out of this deal? Best be up-front right now, son."

Taken aback by the question, Lucas shook his head. "No,

sir. I am not. I'm asking you to explain what we agreed on for me again."

"'Spose I ought to introduce myself if you don't recall." He bowed. "Hector Alvarado, at your service. Back when your daddy was riding broncs, he and I were tight, seeing as we both had a love for the Lord." Hector held up two fingers close together in a sweeping gesture. "I was at his memorial service, though I doubt you recall. Long time ago. Still miss him and your momma."

Lucas nodded, acknowledging the sentiment, and finding himself intrigued and curious about a rodeo friend of his father's. "It's an honor to meet you, sir. Were you a bronc rider as well?"

"Oh no. I'm a bulldogger. Sometimes your daddy worked as my hazer."

From behind Lucas, Trevor cleared his throat, reminding him of his presence. "This is my brother, Trevor. Trev manages the ranch."

"Pleased to meet you." The clanging and squeaking of a horse trailer opening had the men turning. "That's my eldest," Hector said. "Rode with me from Skiatook."

Lucas smiled as Hector's son brought a sorrel mare around the trailer. "So I bought a horse," he said. Every day brought a new surprise. If his life were a novel, no one would believe it was all possible.

Hector nodded. "Paid cash and everything. I've got a copy of your bill of sale in the truck, if you need it."

"No, that's fine. I probably have my copy in the house." With all the other papers in the office that he hadn't read yet.

"Mighty fine-looking animal," Trevor said.

When the mare shook her reddish mane and snorted, Hector's son ran a hand over the animal's flank and murmured soothing words.

"Della is a beauty. Good-natured as well," Hector said. "I

was supposed to have her down to your ranch in August, but I ran into some problems. Like I said, I tried to call. Finally, I gave up. I figured I'd get here when I get here."

"Turns out we both had problems," Lucas said. "My phone bit the dust in the accident. Apologies for the confusion."

"Aw, no problem. I'm here. You're here. And so is Della. All's well."

"You're right," Lucas said.

"Why don't I have Slim Jim take Della to the corral and check her out?" Trevor said.

"Thanks, Trev."

"Slim Jim?" Hector asked.

"Jim is the ranch horse whisperer."

Hector nodded. "As soon as Della is checked, we'll take off."

"Getting dark soon," Lucas returned. "We've a little barbecue party about to start. Why don't you stick around? You're welcome to spend the night in the bunkhouse and head out in the morning."

Hector cocked his head and looked Lucas up and down. "You sure? Don't want to crash a party."

"It's only friends, and you're a friend, Hector." Lucas smiled.

"That's mighty generous of you." The man inhaled and smiled. "I can smell smoked pork on the grill, which means I'd be a fool to say no." The old cowboy glanced around. "You boys have done a fine job with this ranch. Your daddy would be proud."

"Thanks," Lucas said. "It's mostly my brothers."

"Nah," Hector said. "It takes a village." He grinned. "Point me to the bunkhouse and we'll get cleaned up."

"Straight up that path toward the red barn. First building on your left. And when you're ready, follow the path to the back of the house. You can't miss the tents we set up."

"Thank you kindly." Hector tipped his hat and headed over to his son, who waited at the horse trailer.

"Who was that?"

Lucas turned at Sam's voice. "That was a man I bought a horse from. Hector Alvarado. Friend of Dad's. Sound familiar?"

"Yeah, it does. He lived in Homestead Pass for a short time." Sam gave a slow nod. "Well, I'll be. That brings back more than a few memories."

"Such as?" Lucas prompted. Once again, he found himself eager for information about his parents.

"Hector and his wife held a Bible study in their home for a while. Mom and Dad were regulars. I know because I had to babysit you and Trev. I was about fifteen and you two were eleven." He grimaced and shook his head. "Yep, that was around the time you fell out of the hay loft and broke your arm. Good times."

"I was a kid," Lucas protested.

"You sure were." Sam looked at Lucas. "A horse? How does the horse fit into all of this?"

"You tell me." Lucas frowned. "Did Gramps happen to mention the boxes?"

Sam chuckled. "He did."

"There you go. I've ten boxes of merch, a ring, and now a horse. Makes me wonder what else I got myself into."

"You might find out tonight. Are you sure you're ready for that?"

"I don't have any other options. I have a couple dozen questions and zero answers."

"Did you call the jeweler to find out if the clerk that sold you that diamond remembered you?"

"I did. The clerk that sold the ring to me was let go. The owner can't even find the sale in the computer system. He blames it on their new point-of-sale software. Says the transaction has to be in there somewhere and assured me that he'd call me as soon as they figure out what happened." Lucas ran a hand over his face. "I am not feeling reassured."

"Maybe Liv will have some ideas."

"Liv? You told your wife?" Lucas gave his brother a shove. "Does everyone know about my personal problems?"

"She's my wife. We don't keep secrets."

"Why not?"

"Oh, grasshopper, you have a lot to learn."

A guitar twang, followed by the screech of a microphone and the static of a sound system setting up, interrupted the conversation. A moment later, the notes of a familiar country song floated to them from the other side of the house.

Trevor walked across the gravel to rejoin Lucas. "So you hired a band," his brother said. "Anyone I know?"

"I didn't hire a band. Gramps did. Three gals. They're Jane's granddaughters. Call themselves the Dixie Hens. Gramps said they've been on tour with L. C. Kestner."

"Who?" Trevor scrunched up his face and looked at Sam, who shrugged.

"Got me," Lucas said. "Allowing an octogenarian to find the band for a bunch of millennials may not have been my best move."

"Gramps is a man for all generations," Sam said. "Let's give the Dixie Hens a chance."

"Fair enough," Lucas returned.

"So I heard about your plan," Trevor said.

Lucas released a sound of protest as he stared at Sam. "Did you tell the whole world?"

"Aw, cut it out," Trevor said. "I'm your twin. I knew something was up. You should have told me yourself. And if you had, I'd have said this whole idea sounds risky. With your amnesia, there's about a dozen ways to put your foot in your mouth. Bad idea, Luc."

"It's not a bad idea. It's a very efficient plan. Besides, it's

Sam's idea. He's the one who mentioned Cinderella. That prince should have worked smarter, not harder. Gathering all the women I know in one place saves time and money."

"Do not blame me for this fiasco," Sam said.

"It's not a fiasco. And I'd appreciate a little help tonight. I need ears in the crowd. Once the party starts, mingle. You might hear something important."

"You expect us to mingle and chat up twenty single women in front of our wives?" Sam asked. "That is the second dumb thing you've said in ten minutes. Man, you really don't understand women, do you?"

"No. He doesn't," Drew said as he joined them.

"You told Drew too?" Lucas glared at Sam. "Big mouth."

"I forced it out of him," Drew said.

"For the record, I invited the ranch wranglers as well." Lucas shook his head, eager to change the subject. "So have you seen my new horse?"

"And what's with that?" Trevor asked. "Though I will admit Della is a fine animal. Do you need another horse?"

"I'm starting a training school. Makes perfect sense."

"And another thing…" Trevor continued. "How come I was the last to hear about your training school? Good thing Sam keeps me in the loop." Trevor eyed Lucas.

"Trev, I told you I planned to retire first of the year. I also told you I planned to start a training center."

"First of the year is January. This is September. The way I hear it, construction starts soon."

"Since I'm grounded, we moved up the timeline." Lucas shrugged.

"'We'?" Trevor asked.

"Me and Harper," Lucas said.

"You're fortunate to have her on your team," Drew said.

"Oh, she's more than on his team," Sam said. "She's his business partner."

Trevor shook his head and looked at Lucas again. "We need to have a sit-down chat. I've learned more in the last three minutes about my own brother's life than I have in six months."

"Welcome to my world," Lucas said. "I don't know what happened the last six months either."

"Are you able to recall anything?" Trevor asked.

"Not a thing." He shook his head. "I've signed a contract, taken on a business partner, and am about to break ground on my parcel. Can't remember planning any of it."

"If you're using your parcel for the training center, where do you plan to live?" Trevor asked.

"I'm doing fine at the ranch house with Gramps."

"You're gonna live with Gramps forever?" Trevor asked. Both Sam and Drew had amused smiles on their faces.

"Are you trying to make a point here?"

"Yeah, I am. You have a ring and, somewhere out there, you have a future Mrs. Lucas Morgan. She won't want to live at the main house with your grandfather."

"How do you know that? Seems to me like my timing is pretty spot on. You left and got married. I'm there now. Gramps isn't alone in that big house." He looked at Trevor. "Why are you looking for trouble where there is none?"

"I'm just saying."

Lucas shrugged, hesitant to admit that Trevor had a point. What if his bride didn't have warm feelings about the Morgan homestead? The white-clapboard home had been around for over forty years. The place had been added onto more times than he could count. Most women wanted a new modern house when they started their married life.

He kicked at a rock. Nope. Not going there. He had bigger fish to fry right now than worrying about where he and his mystery bride would live.

"I want to know about that horse," Drew said.

"Nothing to know. It's a horse. A man can always use another horse."

"When did you have time to buy a horse since you've been home?" his eldest brother persisted.

"I didn't. I bought it sometime while on the circuit."

In the distance, the sound of vehicles crunching over gravel could be heard. Headlights skipped over the large moss-covered pillars that stood like sentries at the entrance of the ranch drive and lit up the drive as they approached.

"Mind if we finish this conversation later?" Lucas asked.

"Not a problem." Drew pinned him with a look. "We have a lot to talk about."

"Looks like your guests are arriving," Sam said. "You better go get changed."

"I did change." Lucas looked down at his black T-shirt and Wranglers. "Showered too."

"Aren't you going to shave?"

"I shaved yesterday." He ran a hand over his stubble. "If there's a woman out there willing to wear my ring, she likes me just like I am."

"Oh brother." Sam groaned and rolled his eyes. "That's not exactly how Prince Charming works."

Lucas grinned. "It's how Lucas Morgan does."

A luxury sedan parked and a dark-haired woman carefully stepped out of the vehicle. Despite the setting sun, oversize white sunglasses obscured her face. She wore a red blouse, its collar raised, along with a white skirt and red peep-toe shoes. Removing the sunglasses, she moved carefully over the gravel toward him.

"Is that Claire Talmadge?" Drew asked.

"Sure is," Sam said. He gave a nod to the cute brunette. "Didn't she leave for New York to model or become an actress or something?"

"That's what I heard," Trevor added.

"It's showtime, fellas." Lucas waved his brothers off with a hand. "Time for you to disappear."

"Claire Talmadge. Tough job, but someone's gotta do it," Sam said. "Never understood why she gave you a second glance and ignored the handsome Morgan brother. Me."

Drew gave Sam a light smack on the back of the head. "That's because you were head-over-boots in love with Olivia, goofball."

Lucas ignored his brothers as he crossed the yard to meet his old flame. For the life of him, he couldn't pinpoint the exact details surrounding why they'd parted ways. He did recall that while Claire was one of the most beautiful women he'd ever dated, they hadn't had much in common.

"Claire, thanks so much for stopping by."

The brunette smiled and glanced over his shoulder. "Did I scare off your brothers?"

"Nah, they have someplace to be."

Claire put a hand on his arm. The gesture set off the tinkling of a dozen silver bracelets on her wrist. She smiled. "It was so nice to run into you in San Antonio. I told my mom we had dinner. Mom considers you the one that got away."

"I, uh…" Lucas swallowed, panic choking him as he searched for a response. Could Claire be the one?

"You can breathe, Lucas." Claire's laughter trilled. "I think you're wonderful, too, but my fiancé is pretty special."

"You're engaged." Relief hit like a welcome rain.

"A gal can't wait around for Lucas Morgan forever." She raised her left hand and wiggled the fingers to show off a rock the size of Texas.

"Congratulations," he said.

"Thank you." Claire paused. "What about you? As I recall, you mentioned a special woman on your mind that evening."

Lucas did a double take at the comment. "I did?"

"Yes. Though you never said who it was."

They chatted for a few minutes and when Claire sashayed off to the party, Lucas spent a few minutes trying to recall dinner with the brunette. Dinner where he'd mentioned another woman.

Ninety minutes later, the party was in full swing and Lucas did the math. He'd ruled out ten of his twenty female guests. He'd tried to locate Harper, but every single time he tried to find her, another of his former girlfriends managed to corner him for a one-on-one chat. He may have lost a chunk of memory and couldn't recall the names of a few of them, but the reason why some of these women were exes came back to him within a few minutes of conversation.

"Lucas!" a singsong female voice called out.

He turned to see a perky redhead in a short-sleeved plaid shirt, Wranglers and cowboy boots approach. A redhead he'd never seen before in his life. Her long strawberry hair swung, kissing her shoulders as she walked his way.

She grinned. "I'd say long time no see, but I did see you at the Lawton rodeo."

"Lawton," Lucas murmured. That was where he'd left six months of his life along the roadside. He prayed the deer fared better.

"It was so lovely of you to invite me. How are you doing? I heard you hit your head pretty hard."

He glanced down at her and squirmed. Was she really batting her eyelashes? "You know me. Hardheaded."

"Did you get the flowers I sent?"

"Sure did. Thank you." Her flowers had to be among the dozen or so arrangements delivered from the Elk City florist.

"That's why I decided to have this shindig," Lucas continued. "To thank everyone for their kindness. A man finds out who his friends are when he's laid out."

"This is very generous of you. I was more than surprised to get that message inviting me. How did you get my number?"

"I called the florist and asked them to reach out to you."

A phone started ringing and Lucas glanced around.

"Your phone is ringing."

"Is that mine?" Lucas chuckled. "Guess so." He pulled his device from his pocket and stared at the screen. *Harper.* "If you'll excuse me a moment, I better take this." With a nod, he stepped away from the redhead.

"This is your friend Harper saving you from Ginny Malone."

"Who?" he asked.

"Ginny Malone. Trick rider. That's the woman you're chatting with. We met her in Lawton in August. Be careful. She's half in love with you and only needs a bit of encouragement to push her over the line."

"Oh?" Lucas looked back at the redhead and offered an awkward smile when she cocked her head and batted her eyelashes again. "*Oh!* That's not good." He glanced around again. "Where are you?"

"Over by the band."

Lucas eyed the band area where Harper stood next to the makeshift stage. She grinned and waved at him.

"You better get back to Ginny," she said. "Let her down easy, Lucas."

Let her down easy? He couldn't recall who she was. The only thing he was sure of was that the redhead was not the woman who held his heart. No way. No how.

It took a good fifteen minutes to convince Ginny that he couldn't come to Lawton to visit her next week. By the time he'd directed her interest to the dessert table, Harper was nowhere to be found.

"Having fun?" Gramps asked. His grandfather sidled up next to him with a can of Dr Pepper in his hand.

"Define fun," Lucas asked.

Gramps chuckled. "This was your idea."

"So it was." The night wasn't a total failure. It was good to see his friends and former girlfriends. Though, so far, he didn't have a clue who the woman he'd fallen in love with could be.

"Appreciate you letting your brothers help with the party."

Lucas turned and looked at his grandfather. "Huh?"

"You let them help you. Normally, you're all about doing everything yourself."

"Am I?" He frowned, letting that information sink in.

"Yep. Nice of you to invite Hector and his son to the party too."

"Friend of Dad's. Seemed like the right thing to do." Lucas glanced at his grandfather once again. "Did you know Hector back then?"

"Ran into him a time or two. 'Course, I was living in Tulsa when your daddy was on the circuit."

Lucas nodded, his scrutiny spanning what he could see of the ranch in the moonlight. The silhouette of the old barn stood out against the black-velvet night sky. Hector was right. His daddy would be proud of how his brothers had built up the Lazy M. The ranch was their father's legacy. Once again, Lucas asked himself what his legacy would be.

"Your brothers are having a good time on the dance floor," Gramps observed. "Good for them to get out without the kids on occasion."

He looked in the direction of the band. Drew and Sadie, Sam and Liv, and Trevor and Hope all moved to the slow strains of a ballad. Lucas's heart clutched at the sight. He longed for what his brothers had.

"Here comes Harper," his grandfather murmured.

Harper walked across the grass, illuminated by the overhead lights that Sam and Drew had strung from the tent to the path leading to the drive. His eyes followed her the entire time. She wore a peach dress that swished around her legs as she moved. When their gazes connected, Harper's mouth lifted in a sweet smile that warmed him.

There was something comforting about his old friend's presence. Something that said everything was going to be all right.

"Doesn't she look pretty tonight?" Gramps continued.

"Yeah. Real pretty," Lucas murmured, surprised at the thud of his heart. For a moment all he could think about was how she'd felt in his arms when she'd nearly killed herself on those steps at the cabin.

"Maybe you oughta think about falling for someone like Harper," Gramps said.

"Harper?" Lucas blinked. "We're just friends."

"Keep telling yourself that," his grandfather said. The elder Morgan began to wander in the direction of the band.

"Where you going, Gramps?"

"Going to find someone to chat with who doesn't need glasses." He waved a hand. "Make sure you talk to that eye doc about your vision problems."

"I have."

Gramps shook his head. "You're not getting any better, son. I'll be praying."

Lucas chuckled. Once Gramps got an idea in his head, he hung on to it like a dog with a bone.

Fact was, there was nothing he'd like more than to find someone like Harper. Sweet, smart and beautiful.

That person didn't exist and, as he reminded himself half a dozen times, there was no way he'd cross the line and ruin the special friendship between himself and Harper.

Harper reached Lucas as the band started its second set of the night. The song was the cover of a popular romantic country ballad. A warm breeze mussed her hair and she pushed the long locks away from her face. She eyed the dance floor where twinkling lights woven through the trees cast a soft glow on the event as the cowgirls and cowboys paired up.

"Are you dancing tonight?" Harper asked.

"Ah, no." Luc's eyes were shuttered as his gaze skimmed over her. He ran a hand across his face and nodded. "Nice dress."

Harper took his expression as a positive indicator. Lucas rarely commented on her appearance. Maybe his hit on the head had changed that. She could only hope he'd start seeing her as a woman and not just his buddy.

"I got it at that little boutique across the street from Sam's shop, next to the bookstore. Glitz and Glam."

Realizing that all of Luc's exes would be here tonight, she'd gone into the boutique and bought an overpriced stunner of a dress. She refused to give up without a fight. Once upon a time, she and Lucas had connected. Harper had waited a long time to see tenderness reflected in his eyes. Maybe what she saw tonight was more than tenderness. Whatever it was, she hadn't imagined it.

"Are you having fun?" Harper asked.

"You're the second person to ask me that." Luc smiled. "I'm enjoying the food. That's for sure. Did you try the mac and cheese? Loretta says it's a blend of Asiago and Cheddar. I want to know what the crunchy stuff on top is."

Harper looked up at him. Sometimes he was so dense. "I'm not talking about the food, Luc."

"What are you talking about?"

Suddenly irritated, Harper waved a hand around. "This reality show you staged. Was there some kind of plan here inviting all your girlfriends? I mean besides the excuse of needing to return their dishes?"

Lucas shrugged and looked away. "Yeah, there was. I can't remember stuff, Harper. Important stuff." He cleared his throat. "I've spoken to nearly all the women here...well, except the ones that got married or engaged in the last six months."

"Are you going to get to the point soon?"

"Did you happen to notice…? I mean… Did I say something that might lead you to believe that I was maybe seeing one of these ladies before I lost my memory?"

Harper groaned aloud as she clenched and unclenched her hands. "No, Lucas, you did not. We've discussed this before. I do not keep track of your love life."

His eyes popped wide at her response. "Easy there. Just asking."

"And I'm just telling."

"Whoa. I'm sorry. It wasn't my intention to annoy you, Harp." He took her hand and held it gently. "I apologize."

He looked down at her, concern in his blue eyes, his lips a worried line. His caramel-colored hair curled at the nape of his neck and the stubble on his angular face had her itching to lay her palm on his cheek.

"Fine." She pulled her hand free from the torture of touching his. "Try to remember that I'm here to support you, and not to analyze your love life."

"Okay, got it. No talk about women." He offered a half smile. "Let's start over. How about if we chat about horses?"

"Horses. You're going to have to be more specific than that. Why do you want to talk about horses?"

"A fella from Skiatook just delivered a pretty mare. I bought her a few months ago. Turns out, he was a friend of my father's."

"You bought a horse."

Luc sighed. "Yep. I bought a horse, just like I bought the pens and mugs and other merch."

"You don't remember buying this horse?"

"Nope."

"Well, you were going to have to pick up a horse or two once the training center opened."

"Yeah, there is that. Except if my timeline is correct, I purchased the horse when I thought the center would open next spring."

"True," Harper said with a nod. "Did you know this fella was a friend of your father's before you bought the horse? I mean it probably doesn't matter in the scheme of things, but you have to wonder."

"Hmm." Luc cocked his head and rubbed his chin. "That's an excellent question. I don't know." He nodded at the grills. "Hector Alvarado. That's him, with the big smile, talking to Gramps."

Harper's eyes followed Luc's to where Gus Morgan and an older cowboy stood deep in conversation.

"I'll ask him."

"Luc, wait. I want to meet your horse."

"Stop by tomorrow after church?"

"Sure."

"Great." His smile broadened. "Now, don't go away. I'm going to talk to Hector and then I'll find you."

Harper nodded. *Do that, Luc. Find me.*

He walked away and her gaze followed him. Would she always be following Luc? Attending this party was a terrible idea.

Maybe her father was right and she was fooling herself. After fourteen years of friendship, was she simply another Lucas Morgan buckle bunny, hoping for his attention, pretending to herself she meant more to him?

"Some things never change. Do they? Lucas Morgan is as handsome as ever."

"What?" Harper spun around at the comment. "Jackie! I didn't expect to see you here. What a nice surprise." The tall, smiling brunette had been Harper's close friend in her early days on the circuit, as they were both from Oklahoma. Over the years, their paths had crossed less and less, a regrettable result of their nomadic lifestyle.

"I heard through the circuit grapevine that Lucas won't be going back to bronc riding. I had to stop by."

"He'll be thrilled to see you." Harper smiled. "What about you? Are you still team roping? I heard you won in Vegas last year."

"Can't do it forever. One more year and then I'll retire." She shrugged. "I always feel a pull to settle down come autumn. The leaves turn and the air smells like change. I long to find a place of my own to burrow into. My partner retired, which compounds things. I don't suppose you'd be interested in joining me part-time next year."

"I might be. Everything is up in the air right now," Harper returned. "Luc and I are working on a training center. We'll be hiring instructors come early spring, and the facility will allow for private instruction. Maybe I could give you a call when things fall into place and I know my schedule with the training center."

"Do that, and think about roping, will you?" The other woman grinned. "If you have time with being the president of the Lucas Morgan fan club and all."

"Am I?"

"It's pretty much common knowledge."

"I guess there are worse things," Harper said with a laugh. Except it wasn't funny. Not at all. She didn't want to be the needy woman in the shadows waiting for crumbs from Luc's table and she sure didn't like the idea that was what others saw when they looked at her. "Mind if I ask you a personal question, Jackie?"

"Go for it."

"Why did you and Luc break up? You dated for a while, as I recall."

"Luc's a great guy, but I can't say he ever let me see past that charming smile. I wanted more." Jackie lifted a shoulder. "Luc is one hundred percent wonderful, but he holds back. What he's thinking, what he's feeling."

Harper nodded. The words were a fair assessment, though

she had been allowed to see behind the curtain a few times. Luc wore a mask that he rarely removed. The emotion he'd shared at the cabin after the Kids Day Event had been rare. Would he ever drop his guard completely?

"I'm guessing you're closer to him than anyone," Jackie said.

"We're friends. If that's what you mean."

"Oh, don't sell yourself short, Harper." The other woman offered a kind smile. "You mean much more than that to Luc."

Harper remained silent, unmoved by Jackie's words. She meant a lot to him, but not in the way she'd hoped.

Jackie stepped closer and peered at Harper. "Oh my. You're in love with him, aren't you?"

She looked at her friend and nearly crumbled as the question hit the target with surprising accuracy. Jackie cut through all the layers of excuses Harper so readily spouted day after day, year after year.

"Is it so obvious?"

Jackie nodded, her smile gentle. "Have you thought about telling him how you feel?"

Harper swallowed. "If I tell him, I run the risk of losing his friendship."

"Maybe it's worth the risk, Harper. You can't go on in this limbo forever."

"You're right." Harper sighed. "You're absolutely right." It occurred to her that Jackie's insight wasn't much different than her father's. The difference was that her friend had been there and done that and knew what it felt like.

Silence stretched between them for a minute as forlorn strains of a ballad filled the air.

"So you two are starting a training center. That's why you're back in Homestead Pass," Jackie said.

"I'm working with my father short-term and planning the training center with Luc. Like you, I'm trying to figure out what to do with the rest of my life."

"A lot of that going around." A woman's laughter rose above the chatter of party guests. Jackie turned to Harper, brows raised. "Claire Talmadge is here?"

"Yes, she's in town visiting her folks."

"This is like old home week, isn't it? Remember how the three of us used to run around?"

What Harper recalled was that Luc had dated all her friends.

"I'm going to go give Claire a hello and find Lucas."

"Do that, and don't forget to check out the buffet."

"I will." Jackie squeezed Harper's hand. "Hang in there, honey."

"Oh, that's my specialty."

For minutes, Harper replayed what Jackie had said. When the band burst into a fun tune, she began to tap her toes.

"Nice party." Harper turned to find Slim Jim, the ranch horse whisperer, standing nearby with a soda in his hand.

"It is. Do you want to dance?" she asked.

Jim dropped the soda and stumbled while working to pick up the can as it spewed its contents. "I, uh… Not right now. Thank you."

Harper's jaw sagged at the cowboy's response. Deer in the headlights was an understatement.

"What is with that look?" she asked. "Am I repulsive or something?"

"No, ma'am. You look fine. It's Luc. I don't want to get him mad at me."

"Luc? What does Luc have to do with me asking you to dance? Maybe you didn't get the memo. Luc and I are friends. Best buds. Amigos."

"That may very well be true, but I don't think he'd be a fan of me dancing with his friend."

"Is that right?" Harper's breath came out in short staccato bursts as she worked to control her anger.

"I gotta go." Jim raised his palms and started to slowly back up. "I'm pretty sure my mother is calling me."

"Your mother?"

"Yes, ma'am. If she's not, she ought to be. I told myself I was going to keep out of trouble this month, and you're not helping matters."

Harper looked around for Luc and spotted him standing with a woman on either side of him, a grin splitting his face. She turned on her heel and headed down the drive toward her truck. It was time to end this fun and games. She was so over being Luc's sidekick.

It was time for her to prayerfully make decisions about her future. A future that didn't include waiting on Lucas Morgan.

Chapter Eight

Lucas leaned against the corral fence. Inside the fence, Slim Jim worked with Della. The animal allowed Jim to rub her neck and add a rope halter. Jim walked the mare through a series of exercises. Each time the animal proved to be docile and cooperative. Perfect for training students at the soon-to-be training center.

Pulling out his cell phone, Lucas called Harper again. For the third time, it went to voice mail, so he tried texting.

Looks like you aren't coming by to see my horse. Let me know if you're okay or I'll have to come looking for you.

Harper's response was immediate.

Sorry. Busy day. I'll catch you later.

"Who're you texting?" Sam angled himself around from his perch on the top rung of the fence, doing his best to peek at the screen of Lucas's phone.

"Harper. She was supposed to come by after church."

"I heard she left the party early last night. Jim said she was upset about something."

Lucas glared at his brother. "Remember how I explained that Harper and I don't discuss our personal romantic business?"

"Yeah."

Lucas shoved the phone back in his pocket. "Thanks to your advice, I tried to pick her brain about that very topic. It didn't go well at all."

Sam pushed back the brim of his hat and shook his head. "Uh-uh. That's not my fault. I said you don't know a thing about women, and I stand by that statement."

"Me? Your idea. Your fault."

"Nope. I warned you before you sent out invitations to that train wreck."

"It wasn't a train wreck. I figured out that not a one of those women from my past were in the running for my future."

When Cooper and Patch, two of the family ranch dogs, barked and whined, Trevor and his son, Cole, turned from the fence to see what the fuss was.

"Lower your voice," Trevor said. "You're upsetting the dogs and spooking the horse."

"What are you two arguing about anyhow?" Drew asked.

"Discussing. Not arguing," Sam said. "Lucas is in hot water with Harper."

"I don't know that for sure," Lucas said.

"I think she's mad at you," Sam continued.

"Not surprised."

Lucas turned to Drew. "What's that supposed to mean?"

"It means you can't invite nearly two dozen women to a party without expecting some fallout."

"That's not a fair assessment," Lucas protested. The party hadn't provided the results he'd hoped for. However, chatting with his guests had filled in a few more details on his activities over the last six months. That had been helpful.

"Well, boys, we're heading out," Hector called. "Thanks for the hospitality and good food. It was a pleasure to sit in the pew and listen to Pastor McGuinness again."

Lucas and his brothers turned at the words.

"Thank you for bringing Della to the ranch, Hector." Lucas offered a handshake.

"My pleasure." Hector looked from Drew to Sam and then to Trevor and Lucas. "Your daddy would be proud of what you and your brothers have built here on this ranch. As I recall, when he left the circuit, your father was about Luc and Trevor's age with a pocket full of dreams. You and your brothers have kept those dreams alive. This place will be here for generations."

Lucas and his brothers were solemn at Hector's impactful words. They waved as the older cowboy and his son drove off, pulling the horse trailer behind their dually. The empty trailer clanged rhythmically as it moved over the gravel drive.

"Wow, that man sure put everything in perspective, didn't he? I forget that the ranch isn't just our job. It's our legacy. It all started with Mom and Dad. Now the Morgans have doubled. A powerful reminder of how a dream can start out small and grow, touching so many lives," Drew said.

"Reminds me of the parable of the mustard seed," Sam said.

"Exactly," Drew responded.

For a moment, Lucas let the words roll over him. Would it be the same with the training center? Would his dream grow into a reality that blessed others? He sure hoped so.

"How did you find Hector anyhow?" Trevor asked.

"I asked him the same thing. He didn't know, and I can't recall." Lucas shrugged.

The response had Drew frowning. "That has to be frustrating."

"Tell me about it."

"What do the doctors say about your memory?" Trevor asked.

"The usual. My memory is a waiting game."

"You know…" Sam said with a grin. "In the movies, a hit

on the head always restores memories when someone has amnesia. Happy to oblige, Luc."

Lucas ignored Sam and turned to Trevor. "I'll be cleared to drive as soon as I complete therapy. Hopefully, in a week or two. I'm not holding my breath on the horseback riding."

"Hey, you got time," Trevor returned. "You said early spring is the target to open the facility. A lot can happen in six months."

"Yeah. A lot has happened in the last six months."

"True that," Trevor said. "Did I see excavation going on at the construction site?"

"Yeah. They'll be laying foundation rebar and column starter bars soon."

Construction had begun. He couldn't believe he was saying those sweet words. Yet somehow things felt off without Harper sharing the milestone.

"How about if we all go check it out?" Drew asked.

"Good idea," Trevor said with a nod. "I'll take the pickup and bring Cole and the dogs."

"Wait up," Sam said. "I'll go with you, Trev."

"Let's grab a UTV." Drew nodded to Lucas. "You can ride shotgun."

"I've got news for you," Lucas groused. "Shotgun is my life now."

A short time later, his brothers walked the construction area, interest evident on their faces. Excitement and pride stirred in Lucas's gut as he explained the project details and Sam and Trevor asked questions.

"This is where the outdoor arena will be." Lucas pointed to the area marked off with string and flags where trees had been removed to be transplanted elsewhere on the property. He glanced around, imagining a sunny day, the air filled with the scents of popcorn, horses and dirt. The arena would be filled with cheering spectators when the First Annual Homestead Pass Training Center Rodeo began opening ceremonies. In his mind's eye he saw Harper leading barrel racers while he took over as the arena announcer as the festivities began.

"You already have an inside arena planned," Sam said. "Wouldn't a corral work as well and be a whole lot cheaper?"

"Nope. An arena outside gives us options for future growth. When we open, we don't have to expense seating right away. If we decide to launch a rodeo-type event as a conclusion to training sessions, it'll work well. It'll also be good for anyone interested in the training center in the future."

"He's right," Trevor said. "It's cheaper to do it now than to drag equipment in here at a later date."

"Think of it as another passive income opportunity. We can rent out the space too."

"When did you get so smart?" Sam asked.

Lucas looked at Drew. "Wasn't me. It was Drew."

"Nope." Drew gave an adamant shake of his head. "Not me. This was all Harper's planning. She hired the first architect. Most everything had been researched when I picked up the ball."

"Maybe you oughta find out why she's mad at you," Trevor said. "Sounds to me like Harper is a partner you don't want to lose."

Yeah, Trevor was right. Lucas had realized that, when the bank loan had been approved, he'd better adjust to the fact that Harper was the brains of the operation.

Just the same, he glared at Sam.

Something was up with Harper and what he was going to do about the situation was the question.

"Send her flowers," Trevor said as though reading his mind. "A dozen roses will cover a lot of missteps. Trust me, I know."

Lucas nodded, mulling Trevor's suggestion. Yeah, flowers might be a good idea, but not roses. Harper wasn't a roses kind of gal. He'd ask Bess. She'd know.

"Whether she's mad or not, you oughta thank her for her support," Drew added.

Drew was right. She had supported him through all this and, in return, he'd been a big jerk about the partnership issue.

Sam walked to the cabin. He crouched down, assessing the building from different angles. "What's going to happen here? Looks like one strong gust of wind and this place will be kindling."

"Nah," Lucas said. "It's solid. Needs a little work, is all."

"A little work?" His brother grinned. "If you say so. Want some help?"

"No. I got it."

Sam's expression said he was doubtful. He opened his mouth as if to offer more advice and then closed it again.

"That cabin sure has some good memories," Trevor said.

"For Drew and me as well," Sam said.

"Dad brought you two up here?" Lucas asked.

"Yep. You two were only babies when Dad started the tradition." Drew nodded to Lucas. "You had colic. I suspect Dad needed a break. Or maybe Mom did. Dad would grab sleeping bags, drive on up here, and we'd camp."

Sam eyed Lucas. "It's possible you still have colic."

"Real funny," Lucas said. His gaze spanned the area as he recalled what the finished project would look like. "Think Dad would approve of the training center?"

"Approve?" Drew laughed. "I'm surprised he never thought of it himself."

"Yeah?"

"Lucas, this is nearly as solid a plan as the Lazy M Ranch," Drew said. "I'm assuming you'll invite your brothers to teach at your training center."

"I didn't think you'd be interested," Lucas returned, dumbfounded at his brother's comment. He hadn't ever entertained the possibility that they'd be so enthusiastic.

"Are you kidding? Between us, you've got three bronc riders and a bulldogger. Whatever you need, we'll be here for you."

"Don't forget Jim," Trevor said. "He could teach a class or two on his horse whispering techniques."

"Yeah. Okay, I like what I'm hearing. I'm guessing Harper will too."

"When will this be finished?" Sam asked.

"Drew's buddy is our contractor, and barring bad weather, we should be done by the end of the year. Ready to start classes in the spring."

Lucas looked at the cement foundation of the indoor arena building, his gaze taking in the land and the trees before finally settling on his brothers and his nephew.

"The training center name has already been registered. But what do you think about naming the outdoor arena after Dad?"

He looked at each of his brothers. In turn, a grin lit up their faces.

"Gus Morgan Jr. Arena," Lucas murmured. Emotion caught him by surprise and he swallowed hard.

"Ha! I love it," Sam said. "More importantly, Gramps will too."

"Let me run it by my business partner," Lucas said.

"Think Harper will mind?" Trevor asked.

"Nah. She gets what this is all about."

"How'd you get Harper to go into business with you anyhow?" Sam asked. "I always thought she was smarter than that."

Lucas gave Sam a shove. "I don't have a clue. But it's a sore subject, so don't bring that up either."

"What do you mean 'sore subject'?"

He stared at Sam. "I'll explain when I figure it out. Like everything else that happened in the last six months, the details are a little fuzzy."

"Okay, but your business partner is currently mad at you," Sam persisted. "Did I get that part right?"

"Maybe. But, if she is, Harper never stays mad for long. I'm not worried."

Except, he was. She'd avoided him for an entire week. That wasn't normal. Harper was real good about letting him know if there was a problem between them. Things felt different this time, and he didn't understand why. So yeah, he was worried.

Harper slowed the truck at the sight of the Homestead Pass town limits.

"How's Lucas?" her mother asked from the passenger seat. "You haven't mentioned him at all lately."

"I've been pretty busy." She snuck a peek at her mother. The query seemed oddly random.

"Too busy for your best friend? That's a first."

"I saw him at that barbecue party at his house." Harper reached for her sunglasses and slid them on.

"Today is Saturday. That was a week ago. You haven't chatted about the training center either. Have you visited the construction site this week? Didn't Edgar mention breaking ground?"

Edgar again.

"There's nothing for me to do at the training center, Mom. Construction is underway. Drew is an architect. He's Luc's resource person."

"I disagree. If you're a partner, you ought to be at the construction site. This isn't like you, Harper."

"Mom, I thought you and Dad were opposed to me being in business with Luc."

"You're father's simply upset that you aren't feasting at his table."

"What does that mean?"

"He was so sure you'd fall in love with the family business.

I think he's more hurt than anything." Her mother paused. "I've explained to him that this training center project is a good thing because it keeps you close by, and it makes you happy."

"Aw, thanks, Mom."

"Now, about Luc. The man sent you flowers. A lovely gardenia plant. And you haven't said a thing about what's going on. Why would he send you apology flowers?"

Harper gasped. "You looked at the card."

Her mother picked a spec of lint off her black slacks and primly folded her hands in her lap. "Of course I did. I'm your mother." She shrugged. "Clearly, you two had a falling out."

"We didn't. Not really. I've simply decided to step back a bit while I make decisions about my future."

The party had been a wake-up call. Things were all messed up, and it was her fault for expecting more from Luc than he could give right now. The barbecue had made her realize that she had to let go of the notion he'd ever feel the same about her. That ship sailed when he'd hit his head and forgot six months of his life. And hers.

It was time to slip back into the role of Luc's pal and forget about what happened before he'd hit his head.

Could she do that? Could she let go of what might have been? Ignore the longing in her heart that said Luc was the one?

The only way that would work was for her to set a few boundaries.

"Are you listening to me, Harper?"

"What?" Harper's gaze slid from the road to her mother and back again.

"I asked if he'll still be attending Dana's party?" her mother asked.

"I haven't uninvited him, so I suppose he's still coming." The party. She forgot about the anniversary party.

"It seems very odd that you went into business with Luc and now you seem to be backpedaling on the project and him."

Harper gripped the steering wheel tightly. "I am not backpedaling. I have a short-term interning position at Reilly Pecans, just like everyone wanted. I work nine-to-five, five days a week. I don't have time to micromanage Luc."

"You've always multitasked in the past."

"I'm not as young as I used to be," Harper said.

At that, her mother chuckled. "Oh, that's nonsense. I heard you on the phone. You've still got your finger in the pie with your rodeo friends. Do you plan to take off to compete one of these weekends?"

Harper groaned loudly. "Mom. I can't believe you eavesdropped. I expect that from Dad but not from you."

"You were right there in the kitchen talking loud enough for the housekeeper to hear. I can't help it if I overheard as well."

"I haven't made any decisions about the rodeo. That was my friend Jackie on the phone. I ran into her at the barbecue party. A mutual friend is getting married in two weeks. The wedding happens to coincide with a rodeo."

"Really? A wedding that coincides with a rodeo? They planned it that way?"

"It was sort of a spontaneous decision."

"Spontaneous." Her mother cocked her head. "Dana's wedding was two years in the making. Maddy's eighteen months. You aren't going to have your wedding at a rodeo, are you?"

"My wedding?" Harper grimaced. "I haven't had a date in months. You don't have to worry about marriage. Although, I can say with certainty that when I do get married, it won't be an event two years in the making."

"Now, now. Let's not disparage Dana. Your sister's quirks are what make her unique. Just like yours are. As for your unconventional invitation... Go. It sounds like fun, and you deserve a break."

"I'm thinking about it."

"Where is this wedding-slash-rodeo?

"A small town north of Tulsa. I could leave right after work."

The wedding was an opportunity to chat more with Jackie about replacing her partner. Harper ought to be excited, but she found herself loathe to attend another wedding. It would bring up memories of Trevor and Hope's wedding, and how she'd thought her life was finally making sense, and that she and Luc might have a chance at a future together. A future that didn't look like best buddies.

Only a few weeks ago, she was so full of hope. Now, she wasn't certain about anything. Oh, she knew what she had to do; the problem was that she was loath to do it. Putting distance between herself and Luc might be the hardest thing she'd ever done.

Harper directed the vehicle down Main Street while searching for a parking spot near the post office where a shipment of art supplies waited to be picked up. When she spotted Gus and Luc walking down the street toward Sam's shop, she hit the brakes reflexively.

This was the downside of Homestead Pass. You couldn't get mad at someone and attempt to avoid them, because the town was too small.

Her mother reached a hand to the dashboard to brace herself. "Oh my. What was that? Did you see something in the road?" She leaned forward, glancing up and down the street.

"I might have," Harper offered innocently.

Her mother's gaze landed across the street and she scoffed. "You saw the Morgans on the sidewalk." She sighed and turned to Harper. "What on earth is going on, sweetheart?"

"Nothing." Harper pointed to a parking spot next to the barbershop. "Will that work?"

"That's on the other side of the street and almost to the corner. I have fifty pounds of sculpting clay at the post office. We have to park closer to the post office."

"Okay. Fine. I'll find something closer."

Harper dutifully circled the block and backed into a spot right outside the post office.

And as they exited the vehicle, Gus Morgan hailed them with a friendly greeting.

"Great," Harper muttered, grateful for traffic on Main Street that delayed Gus and Luc crossing the street.

Usually, a trip to town was a treat. She'd take a moment to enjoy the beauty of downtown Homestead Pass, the pretty canopied shops and the foliage planted by the town council.

This time of year not only meant pecan harvesting, but it heralded her favorite time of year. Autumn. The trees that lined Main Street would be the first to spread the news of changing seasons and Harper always made a point of assessing them when she came to town.

One or two nights of dipping temperatures would start the redbud leaves turning from green to canary yellow. Soon the maples would shed their summer colors for plum and orange.

Today she eyed the door of the post office and calculated how fast she could dash inside before Gus and his grandson crossed the street.

Too late. The light changed.

"Well, look who we have here," Gus said as they joined them on the sidewalk. He tipped his hat.

Harper checked her phone. Anything to avoid looking at Luc.

"Why, Gus and Lucas, what a timely surprise," her mother said. "I don't suppose you'd mind helping us load a couple of boxes into Harper's truck."

Harper dropped her head to her chest. "I brought a handcart. I can handle the boxes, Mom."

"Luc is happy to help you," Gus said. "Right, Luc?"

"Yes, ma'am. Whatever you need. Happy to help." Lucas nodded and offered Maureen a generous grin. Her mother smiled right back at him as though he could do no wrong.

When had Mom joined Team Lucas? By sending Harper a gardenia plant, Luc had somehow transformed into Prince Charming in her mother's eyes.

"Tell you what?" Gus said. "Why don't we let the youngsters handle those boxes? Have you seen Sam's shop lately, Maureen?"

"I have not, and I've been meaning to. I read that article about his woodcrafts in the newspaper." She took the arm Gus offered and turned to Harper. "You'll need to check the box, dear. We have mail too."

Harper nodded. She was silent as she entered the post office and picked up the mail. Luc was right behind her, watching her beneath hooded eyes. When the clerk brought out two boxes, Harper and Luc reached for them at the same time. Harper quickly jumped back and let him slide the handcart beneath the cardboard.

"You aren't supposed to lift. One of those has fifty pounds of clay and is very heavy," she commented.

Luc ignored her and rolled the boxes out the door and to the truck. "We can do it together. Teamwork. You remember teamwork. Right, Harper?"

"Whatever."

"Whatever?" He arched a brow. "We had a meeting with the contractor this morning. You didn't show."

Harper froze. The meeting with the contractor. She totally forgot, though there was no way she would have made it to the Lazy M in time. Sleep had been elusive of late. "You handled it, correct?"

"Yeah, but that's not the point."

"Yes. I get the point. You're calling me out." Harper released a breath. "I'm sorry that I missed the meeting." She paused. "I've been busy." Busy and confused.

"So you say. Mind telling me why you're mad at me? Why you left the party early?"

"It wasn't that early."

"You didn't even tell me you were leaving."

"Luc, you didn't even notice I was gone. I looked around for you before I headed out. You had a woman on each arm and a smile on your face."

"I was trying to be a good host, and you were supposed to be my support buddy."

"You clearly didn't need my support. I hardly saw you," she muttered.

"Is that why you're mad?"

"I'm not mad." She was hurt, and disappointed. Okay, and mad. Mad at herself for allowing herself to fall for a cowboy who would never settle down. Harper lowered the tailgate on her truck and crossed her arms.

"You sure are cranky."

"I am not cranky. However, for the record, if I were cranky, it's a known fact that accusing a cranky person of being cranky only increases the cranky level."

Luc seemed to find that amusing. His eyes sparkled as he looked at her, though he wisely bit back a laugh.

She stared at him. "Are we going to put the clay in the truck or not?"

"Yes, drill sergeant. On the count of three," he said. "One. Two. Three."

Harper lifted her end and they easily slid the box filled with clay inside. Then she picked up the lighter box and tossed it in before closing the tailgate with unnecessary force.

"I thought you were going to come and see the horse," Luc said. He crossed his arms, his stance mirroring hers as he eyed her like she was a petulant child.

"Is there a rush? Some sort of deadline?" Harper asked.

"No. I guess not."

Harper glanced up and down the street as the silence stretched between them. Where was her mother?

"Look Harp, I apologize." He kicked at the cement with the toe of his boot. "I should have been a better host to you. I'm sorry."

She looked at him, softening at the words.

"I was so sure that party would help me figure things out. I guess all I can do is pray and wait for my memory to come back. Until then, I'm grasping at anything that might help me break through this black void. If I messed up, I'm really sorry."

Harper stared at him long and hard. If only she could tell him that when he'd lost his memory, she'd lost everything as well. Instead, she nodded at his words.

"I, um… I got some news from the eye doctor this week," he said. "Glasses are ordered. I'll be driving soon too."

"Congratulations. I'm happy for you. But you don't have a truck."

"The insurance check showed up. Want to go truck shopping with me?"

She would have jumped at the opportunity to tag along in the past. Spend the day with Luc, looking at trucks.

This wasn't the past. Luc would always be her friend, but the only way to move on was to put a little distance between them.

"Oh, I don't know. I mean you're going to buy another black truck, right? All the same bells and whistles."

"Sure, yeah. I get that. Kind of boring." He paused. "There's something else."

Harper lifted a brow in question.

"I've been talking with my brothers, and I'd like to name the outside arena after my dad." He looked at her, his expression hopeful. "Would that be okay with you?"

"Of course. That's a wonderful idea."

"Thanks." He shoved his hands in his pockets and nodded. "You left the barbecue early. Does that mean I don't have to go to your sister's party with you?" He grinned and wiggled his brows as if hoping to make her laugh.

She wasn't amused. Harper opened her mouth, about to tell him he didn't have to attend. Then she stopped herself. She had purchased a new and expensive dress and spent two and a half hours of her life to support Luc at his ridiculous party. Time that she'd never be able to recoup. And she never even danced. Why should she let him off the hook so easily?

"Seven p.m. sharp."

He groaned and ran a hand over his face.

"You're going to need to shave and get a haircut."

"Aw, come on."

"Proper attire as well."

"Paybacks, huh?" He eyed her. "Could you at least stop by the ranch and meet Della sometime?"

"Della?" Her heart clutched. Another girlfriend?

"The new mare I told you about."

"Oh. The horse. You know what? Let me look at my schedule and get back to you." She couldn't keep running every time Luc called.

"Your schedule?" He raised a brow. "Since when do you use excuses like your schedule?"

"Things have gotten complicated, Luc. I don't know if we can go back to the way things were."

The admission saddened her. Life was about to change whether she liked it or not. Yes, it was time for boundaries if she was going to be able to put the pieces of her heart together and move on.

Chapter Nine

Lucas examined the hors d'oeuvre in his hand and grimaced. Harper was almost back to her old self tonight, so he wouldn't complain about the unidentifiable food at her sister's party. He was grateful they seemed to have moved past the bump in the road of their friendship and knew it would be wise not to overanalyze things.

"Goat-cheese-and-salami-stuffed dates with a bit of honey and pepper," Harper said.

He looked at the cracker, unconvinced. "If you say so. I don't understand why Chef Moretti wants to make this fancy stuff when clearly home cooking is her forte."

"Don't judge. Try it. I promise you'll change your opinion."

He took a bite and his eyes snapped wide as the flavors exploded in his mouth. "Ooh. That's music to my taste buds."

"I told you. Loretta Moretti can do barbecue and haute cuisine. When the Homestead Pass Training Center opens, we'll hire her for the open house."

Lucas chuckled. "You're always six steps ahead of me, Harp. Have you noticed? My brothers sure have."

"Have they?" She shrugged. "It's Reilly Pecans. I'm now officially in the marketing department as assistant to the department head. It has reawakened my creative side. Literally. Sometimes, I wake up in the middle of the night with ideas." She smiled.

"Here I thought the training center was your future. Maybe pecans are."

"My stint with Reilly Pecans will be over in four weeks, Luc. It's been interesting, but the prospect of sitting behind a desk on a regular basis has zero appeal. I'm excited about the prospect of marketing the training center. I'm already working on a social media platform, along with a newsletter. I did some research and talked to a few training schools around the country to see what they're doing that's effective. They were more than willing to answer my questions."

He stared at her. "You're amazing."

"Not really. It's all part of marketing, and I can do it with my laptop sitting in the middle of an arena if I choose." She waved hello at someone across the room.

Lucas followed the direction of her gaze, finding himself counting the number of guests in the Reilly ballroom as he did. "Thought you said this was an intimate get-together. There are at least fifty guests here."

"And they keep arriving." Harper nodded to the doorway where another couple stepped into the room. 'You always knew I wasn't like my sisters. This is more evidence that I'm the cowgirl to their debutante."

"Good thing your father built a mansion with a space that can accommodate a small kingdom. Imagine that. Right here in the middle of Homestead Pass.

She glared at him. "Don't start. Olivia's father has a gated mansion and you don't give her grief."

"That's so the cattle don't escape. And Mr. Moretti's castle is a starter castle compared to your house."

"Not true. It's huge."

"Either way, two wrong millionaires don't make a right."

"What's wrong with a big house?" She took a sip of the soda in her hand as she looked up at him.

"Not a thing. I'm all for big houses filled with kids."

A stunned look raced across Harper's face. "I had no idea you wanted a houseful of children."

"I do. Don't you?"

"Yes. Dogs and cats and a small herd of horses as well." She laughed, choking a little on her soda.

"There you go. We agree on something." He glanced up at the ostentatious crystal chandelier that lit the room. "Bess would never be able to clean that thing."

"We have a service to do that." She reached out and adjusted his tie. "Nice suit, by the way. With that haircut and a shave, you could pass for a banker or an attorney."

"I'm still one-hundred-percent cowboy deep inside." He patted his heart with his palm. "Speaking of attorneys…" Lucas cocked his head in the direction of the buffet table. "I see the House of Usher is here." He nodded at Edgar and Allen. All that was missing was Poe.

Harper burst out laughing. Loud enough to cause her father to turn from his conversation with someone who appeared to be important and shoot her a critical glance.

Lucas nearly laughed himself at the expression on Colin's face. He recognized that look. His father and grandfather had one exactly like it. Lucas had found himself on the receiving end more often than his brothers.

"Oops," Harper murmured. "I'm in trouble again."

"Welcome to the club." He nodded at her sisters' spouses once again. "What do you think the boys are talking about?"

"The stock market or golf. Did I mention that Edgar threw me under the bus at dinner a few weeks ago? He told the family about our project."

"You did." Lucas shrugged. "They had to find out eventually, right?"

"Yes, but…"

Lucas glanced down at her and a light bulb lit up. "You

said your father was furious. It's because you've gone into business with me, isn't it?" He sighed when she didn't answer.

That explained Brett, Allen's cousin, another attorney, whom Lucas now realized had been invited for Harper. He shot a glance at the tall, serious fella talking with Dana.

Lucas didn't like the guy. Not one bit. He was too smooth, and he reeked of eau de money in his bespoke suit and shiny wingtip shoes. Yeah, good old Brett could definitely keep Harper in the Reilly tax bracket. That thought bristled Lucas.

Earlier in the evening, when introductions had been made, Brett had claimed he had always been fascinated by barrel racing. That had kept him and Harper conversing at length while Lucas had considered ways to legally get rid of the guy. He'd barely resisted rolling his eyes at Brett's inane questions about horses.

When he'd noticed Colin across the room, nodding as he observed his daughter and the attorney chatting, Lucas had dialed back his ego to see the situation from her father's eyes.

Brett would fit right in with the family and Harper's plan to settle down.

Could someone like the slick attorney make her happy? It wasn't his place to make that determination. The thought caused a tightness in his chest. It seemed with each day he was coming closer and closer to losing his friend. The strange stirrings in his heart when he considered the inevitable left him confused.

"Lucas, so lovely to see you here."

He turned to see Harper's mother, Maureen, and smiled. He genuinely liked the woman. Most of the time, a ball cap hid her blond hair, and she wore linen smocks with as many pockets as clay stains.

Tonight, she looked like the moneyed matriarch that she was. She wore a sleek black dress, and her hair was expertly coiffed and adorned with a silver clip. A glimpse at Maureen foreshadowed what Harper would look like in a couple of decades. Even more beautiful than today.

For a passing moment, Lucas tried to imagine himself and Harper decades from now. Old friends exchanging witty repartee. Would he always wonder if there could have been more between them?

More between them. Lucas nearly jerked back at the unexpected question that hit him between the eyes. Where had that come from?

They were just friends. A mantra he'd repeated over and over again over the years. So what had changed, leaving him longing for more? Could it be the whack on the head he'd sustained?

"You look lovely, Mrs. Reilly. Thanks for inviting me. I hear you're working on a top-secret project these days."

Maureen chuckled. "All my projects are top-secret. It's the only way to keep my darling husband from coming in every five minutes asking if I've seen his glasses or golf socks."

"Good plan. I ought to try that with my brothers."

"You won't tell anyone. Will you?"

Lucas crossed his heart with a finger. "Your secret is safe with me."

"Good. Now that we are coconspirators, you can tell me all about your and Harper's business. How did that develop?"

"Truthfully, Mrs. Reilly, I don't remember how that happened, so I can't tell you much."

"You're still having memory issues?"

"I've lost six months of my life." He raised a palm. "One minute, I'm on the circuit planning to open a training center when I retire in January. The next, I'm in a hospital bed and I've a business partner, a thousand pens and a new horse."

Along with an engagement ring. That part he would not mention. He already sounded pathetic.

"A thousand pens?"

"Long story."

"I see." She clucked her tongue and sipped her sparkling water as though she did see, which Lucas found comforting. Now he understood where Harper got her empathetic side from.

"You aren't happy about the situation?" Maureen asked.

"The pens?"

She laughed. "I meant having Harper as your partner."

"I'm adjusting." He rubbed his chin, debating how much he should say. "I don't know how much Harper has told you about the circuit, but she's a rising star, and I don't want to stand in her way."

"She doesn't discuss the rodeo much with her father and me. I generally have to eavesdrop if I want to know anything."

"Yeah, well, since we're sharing secrets, I'll tell you that she's had a few small endorsement deals. Each one a little better than the next. I wouldn't be surprised if she were the next face of Lady Bootleg." He leaned closer. "I heard a rumor she's on the shortlist."

"Excuse me?"

"Bootleg Western Wear. It's a brand of women's fancy Western boots and clothing. They use real barrel riders and ropers to endorse the brand."

"Oh, that sounds like quite a serious opportunity."

"It could open doors. That's for sure, and Harper deserves to have doors opened. She works hard, and she's talented."

"So you don't see her future with Reilly Pecans?"

Lucas chuckled. "I'm smart enough not to go there. All I can say is that I want to see Harper doing what brings her the greatest joy."

"You do care about Harper, don't you, Lucas?"

"Harp has always been there for me."

"She's fortunate to have you in her life. I'm glad you got over your disagreement." Maureen smiled. "The gardenia is lovely. It takes a wise man to send a woman a gardenia."

"You think so?"

"Oh yes. Roses are unimaginative." She looked up at him.

"On another note, how long has your brother Sam been creating those beautiful pieces from wood?"

"A long time, though he's sort of kept it under a bushel until recently."

"He's a talented artist. I'm glad to see him getting the recognition he deserves as he steps into his own."

"Yes, ma'am."

"What about you, Lucas?"

"Me?"

"What do you want to be when you grow up?"

The question gave him pause. "I don't—" He nearly said he didn't want to grow up but reconsidered the joking remark. He'd been playing the jokester for far too long. "I want to share my love of horses and the rodeo with others."

I want to make my daddy proud.

Maureen's eyes met his. "I pray your venture is a success. Especially if it keeps Harper close to home."

"Thank you."

She turned and frowned. "Would you please excuse me, Lucas? Ms. Moretti is flagging me down."

"Yes, ma'am. Good to chat with you. Tell her hello from me."

"I shall." She put a hand on his arm. "It was good to visit with you, as well."

Downing his soda, Lucas searched for a refill. From the corner of his eye, he saw Colin Reilly moving in his direction. The last thing he needed was an interrogation by Harper's father. Thankfully, the tall French doors to the patio were open, inviting guests for a stroll around the pool. Lucas ducked behind a tall potted ficus and slipped outside, where he stepped behind a pillar.

He peeked around the base of the massive column. Colin

continued to peruse the crowd for a minute, frowned, shrugged and turned away.

Whew. Close one. Nope, he wasn't ready for one-on-one with the king of the castle, though he recognized that it was inevitable.

Lucas took a deep breath and relaxed for a moment, his attention going to large round globe lights strung on poles to illuminate the yard around the pool area where the skimmer siphoned water over and over. Tall, narrow fir trees surrounded the pool on two sides, their branches woven with more lights whose reflection shimmered on the surface of the water.

The temperature had dropped once again, as it usually did near the end of September. Another week and it would be October. Would his memory be restored by then?

Turning, he could see Harper across the ballroom. Her auburn hair had been pulled back into a low ponytail with a few loose tendrils framing her face. She wore a dark green dress with a fluttery kind of hem.

He wasn't the only one who noticed Harper looked beautiful tonight. While he watched from the patio, what's his name joined her. A surge of something twisted his gut, once again confusing Lucas. After a moment, he chalked up the feelings to protectiveness. When the attorney's regard moved from her face to her figure, Lucas clenched his jaw, working to remind himself that Harper deserved the best. A fella who loved her unconditionally and appreciated all she had to offer. Trouble was, he wasn't convinced the attorney checked those boxes.

Lucas frowned.

Admittedly, he was a tough critic. But this was Harper.

Harper bit into a cracker as Brett said something. She laughed and then coughed, her face becoming red. Then she stopped coughing and pounded on her chest with an open palm.

Lucas stared, horrified as everything slowed down to half

speed and voices blurred. Edgar and Allen turned from their discussion to see what was going on. Dana cocked her head, confusion on her face. Harper's father, across the room, stared, his face a frozen mask of surprise.

No one moved, even as Harper continued to pound her chest, croaking an unintelligible call for help. The attorney didn't move either.

Lucas shot into the ballroom, knocked over a chair and shoved Brett out of the way to get to Harper, whose pleas had turned into a wheeze as her lips turned a flat shade of blue.

Breathing hard, he circled her waist with his arms from behind. His right hand covered his closed left hand as Lucas delivered a sharp upward abdominal thrust.

Immediately, Harper coughed, dislodging a piece of cracker that flew into the air and landed on Brett's lapel.

A low gasp spread through the guests. Relief and adrenaline had Lucas's pulse throbbing like a drum in his ears. He ran a hand over his face and sent up a silent prayer of thanks.

"You. Saved. My. Life." Harper panted each word.

"Yeah, I guess so," he said. "I'm sure someone would have jumped in there. I just reached you first."

Of course, she'd probably be limp and on the floor by the time anyone else reacted. Lucas shuddered at the thought. He'd taken first aid in high school when one of his best friends had had an anaphylactic reaction to a bee sting. He'd never wanted to go through that helpless feeling again.

As it turned out, that class had come in handy today.

Lucas stepped out of the way of the rush of people now surrounding Harper.

He looked up to see Colin Reilly staring at him a lot less like he wasn't good enough for his daughter.

So, yeah, if it made Harper's father see him through a new lens, which was a plus, though he would have preferred a different approach. One that didn't leave his heart pounding and his hands trembling.

As guests and family continued to crowd close to Harper, verifying she was okay, Lucas retreated to the safety of the pool area unnoticed. He was still shaking when Harper found him minutes later.

"Lucas, you saved my life. Thank you."

He turned and looked her up and down to verify that she really was all right. "Wasn't that part of the buddy contract? Section seven, paragraph two, I believe." Joking was the only way he could deal with what had just happened.

Harper laughed, a squeaky sound.

Lucas stood there, unable to move as it hit him. He could have lost Harper, like he'd lost his folks. Panic welled up inside, clogging his throat and threatening to fill his eyes.

"You going to be okay?" His voice sounded raw to his ears.

"Yes." She nodded. "I need a moment. I'm going to stay here for a bit. Everyone was staring at me inside. I certainly didn't mean to steal the spotlight away from Dana."

"Your sister will survive."

For moments, they stood together yet apart, attention fixed on the tiny ripples that rolled across the water's surface with each passing breeze.

Harper wrapped her arm around herself and he heard a sniffle. He turned to see a single tear trailing down her face. Always strong and capable in any storm, Harper wasn't now. Her green eyes were round with fear.

"Hey, hey. What's going on? Are you okay?"

Wordlessly, she shook her head.

Lucas didn't think. He simply pulled her into his arms.

"That was terrifying," she whispered against his shoulder. Her soft breath touched him through the fabric of his shirt and he held her tighter.

Yeah, it was terrifying. Lucas pressed his lips to Harper's

forehead and whispered soothing words as the scent of her perfume wrapped itself around him. He realized that holding Harper felt like the most natural thing in the world. Like he'd waited his entire life for her to fill his empty arms.

All this time he'd spent pushing her away and denying they were anything but friends. What if he'd been wrong?

Harper raised her head and looked up at him. Her soft lips parted and she sighed. The temptation to touch his lips to hers overwhelmed him and he stepped back, away from the warmth of her body. This wasn't good. Not good at all. And he was more confused than ever.

Leaping over the boundary lines could not only ruin that friendship but complicate their business partnership.

Lucas swallowed.

Maybe it was the emotion of what had happened. The adrenaline high.

Sure. That was it.

He had imagined the tug of emotions and the longing in his heart? Because this was his best friend he was talking about.

You weren't supposed to fall for your best friend. That was definitely not in the rule book.

Yet that's exactly what he felt right now. Like he was falling hard. Lucas's mind raced as he recalled that back home there was a ring waiting for him to figure out whose finger it belonged on. Could it be for Harper?

Harper drained the cold coffee in her cup. She picked at her salad and then pushed it away. A glance at her phone told her that her lunch hour was nearly over. It also reminded her that Luc hadn't answered today's text.

She'd texted him Monday and Tuesday, and he'd offered staccato responses. A single word each time. Yeah. Nope.

Yeah, the plumbing crew had shown up.

Nope, the cabin repair hadn't started.

They'd connected on Saturday after the alarming choking incident, and it had further cemented her belief that she and Luc had a chance at a future.

She hadn't imagined things. That moment of connection hadn't been lost in the abyss of his amnesia.

There was a rightness to being in his arms that she couldn't explain. Harper had seen something in his eyes when he'd looked at her as they'd stood together that said he'd felt the same way.

Unfortunately, now he was avoiding her. That didn't bode well. Maybe he regretted almost kissing her—and she was absolutely certain that he had had been about to kiss her.

"You still insist upon eating with the employees, I see." Dana plopped down across from Harper.

"You're corporate, Dana. I'm not. I prefer to eat with the other regular folks."

Besides, the executive dining room was one of the only areas of the company where the décor had Harper shuddering. From the platinum-colored ceiling to the hanging metal birds flying south for the winter, the room held zero warmth. She suspected Dana had helped with the vision.

"No need to get testy. I'm here to remind you that the chef has prepared the Tuesday special. If you want to miss that, fine by me."

"What's the Tuesday special?"

"Roasted Atlantic Black Bass. He serves it with a potato pancake and horseradish crema." Dana offered a chef's kiss.

Harper glanced at her prepackaged salad. "Maybe next week."

She wasn't ready to join the ranks of the Reilly privileged. Despite her last name, she hadn't earned the right to eat in the executive dining room. However, roasted Atlantic Black Bass might prove to be the tipping point.

"Great. I'll save you a seat. It gets busy in there." Dana

smiled. "So…that was some quick thinking by Lucas on Saturday."

"Yes, it was."

"What did you think about Brett? Allen thought you two looked cute together. Maybe we could double date."

"He's nice enough, but I'll pass on the double dating. Life is busy right now…" Harper hedged. She found it humorous that she hadn't heard from Brett, though he'd insisted on getting her phone number before the incident. She suspected Colin Reilly's daughter had lost her appeal when she'd spit on his Italian-silk suit.

Harper chuckled.

"What's so funny?" Dana asked.

"Nothing." She waved a hand dismissively while recalling the cracker sailing through the air and the expression of horror on Brett's face.

"Earth to Harper."

She looked at Dana. "Huh?"

"I asked how you feel."

"My throat is a little raw, and I think my ribs were bruised when Lucas did the Heimlich. He's stronger than he looks."

"Oh, that Lucas. What a hero. So swoony. Daddy was so grateful. I think he's going to name one of our value-added products after him." Dana grinned. "Lucas Divinity, maybe."

Harper burst out laughing and immediately clutched her middle. "Very funny. Try to remember that you're married. You aren't supposed to notice Lucas Morgan."

"Give me a break. Who doesn't notice Luc or any of the Morgan men? They're all from the same mold. Tall, dark, and delicious. It must be the influence of their grandfather. Gus cuts quite a dashing figure for a man of his age."

"How are you and Allen?" Harper asked. Turning the focus to Dana's favorite topic, herself, always worked as a distraction technique.

"We're wonderful. Except for you nearly dying, it was a fabulous party. Allen surprised me with a trip to Napa Valley next weekend. You should see the itinerary." She sighed. "I love that man."

"I'm happy for you, Dana." While her sister's sappy stories of marital bliss got old after a while, Harper was pleased to see her sister so in love.

"It's our last chance to escape before the triple threat."

"Triple threat?"

"That's what they call it around the office, but don't tell Dad. Thanksgiving, Christmas and New Year's. You haven't been around long enough to appreciate how overwhelming things get over the holiday. I mean you seriously need to stay far, far away from Maddy."

"You're right. Thanks for the reminder. She was a pecanzilla last year. I didn't connect the dots. I thought it was the usual holiday harriment."

"Harriment." Dana chuckled. "Good one. But this is much more. It's what happens when you're the senior vice president, of value-added products. The holidays are a triumphant nightmare for her division. All those gift baskets and new products introduced for the season are a huge responsibility. And Daddy is oblivious because October is the start of harvesting."

Harper nodded. A lifetime of pecan harvesting had taught the Reilly girls that their father would be MIA once the season began. Colin Reilly was hands-on and spent most of October and November in the orchards. By December, he reluctantly allowed his field managers to complete harvesting and marketing, all the while claiming he wasn't a micromanager.

"Anyhow," Dana continued, "we were discussing Luc. I talked to Daddy this morning, and he went on and on about Saturday night. That's all I'm saying."

"It's good that he finally appreciates Luc," Harper said. "Even if it's for the wrong reason."

Dana rested her chin on her hands and eyed Harper. "Are you really his business partner?"

"Yes. Why do you say it like that?"

"You could have everything if you stay with the company, Harper. You'd be a vice president in five years. Why would you want to invest yourself in a rodeo school?"

"First, my life is not lacking." *Except someone to share it with.* "Second, it's not just a rodeo school. I'm really excited about this project."

Harper's phone buzzed on the table. "Speaking of Daddy." She picked up the cell. "Yes, Father dear."

"Harper, I need Lucas Morgan's phone number."

"Why?"

"That's my business."

"If you'd tell me, I might be able to find it for you."

"Harper Elizabeth Reilly. I am your father and your boss. I'd like the number now please."

She groaned. "See, this is exactly why I knew working for Reilly Pecans was a bad idea. You have no boundaries."

"Fine." He paused. "You're probably right. This is a personal matter, and I should leave you out of it. I'll call Trevor Morgan's wife. She won't give me a hard time."

"What was that all about?" Dana asked.

"He wanted Luc's number."

"Why?"

"I don't know." Harper shook her head. "But you know Daddy. He's definitely up to something."

Harper immediately called Luc, but it went to voice mail. She tried again during her afternoon break. He didn't pick up.

Harper eyed the clock on her phone half a dozen times, praying for the day to hurry by so she could call Luc and find out what her father was up to.

At 5:00 p.m., she strode to the parking garage. Her phone

rang as she reached her truck. Harper prayed it was Luc. However, the number was unfamiliar.

"Hello?"

"Harper Reilly? This is Katrina Bednar with Bootleg Western Wear."

"Hi. How may I help you, Ms. Bednar?"

"Our executive committee met last evening, and, by a unanimous vote, we've selected you as the next face of Lady Bootleg, our boots and apparel brand for women."

"I'm speechless and honored."

Bootleg Western Wear. Stay calm, Harper. Stay calm.

"I'd love to hear the details," Harper said.

She nodded as Katrina outlined the publicity appearances associated with the position. When she summarized the financials, Harper dropped her tote bag on the ground and leaned against her truck. "That's quite an offer."

"It's a one-year contract that begins in January with a very rigorous schedule. Though I'm sure you're accustomed to traveling on the circuit. This commitment includes, at minimum, twenty days of travel a month."

Twenty days of travel. Minimum. Katrina was correct. That was as many days as her circuit schedule. Driving from rodeo to rodeo took time. Even if the events were on the weekend, the driving sucked up a lot of miles. The difference was that this included all major holidays. She'd be away from family and friends for the better part of each and every month for an entire year.

On the other hand, an endorsement deal would be a huge opportunity to bring attention to the training school.

"May I have some time to think about your generous offer?"

"Sure. I'll need your decision within thirty days."

For minutes, Harper sat in her truck thinking. The exposure would be great, and so would the money. But would it take her any closer to her goals? Would accepting the offer be in her best interest? She'd be forced to really become that silent partner to Luc that she'd talked about to her parents.

Her phone rang and she jumped, startled by the sound. The screen displayed Luc's number.

"Luc, I've been trying to reach you."

"Sorry, I've been monitoring the contractors. Lots of noise. Must have missed your calls. Um, everything okay?"

Did his voice sound nervous? Or was she imagining that? Was that almost-kiss going to make things awkward between them?

"Has my father reached out to you?"

Then Lucas laughed, and she relaxed.

"He sure did. Your father wants to talk. He invited me to a round of golf at the Elk City country club with Edgar and Allen on Saturday." He paused. "I guess that makes me Poe."

"Golf?" She blinked. "I wasn't aware that you play golf."

"I do not, and I have no plans to play in the future. I suggested lunch at Liv's restaurant on Saturday."

"Oh, that's a good idea." She nodded. "Wait. Wait. Why lunch? What is he up to?"

"He's falling over himself to thank me for saving your life. Even mentioned something about my entrepreneurial spirit."

"Your entrepreneurial spirit."

"Yep. He wants to talk business."

"That sounds promising." She paused. "Be careful, Luc. My father is a shrewd businessman."

"It'll be fine, Harper."

"Will you be around if I stop by to see the progress on the training center Saturday? I mean after you have your lunch date?"

"You sure you can squeeze me into your schedule?"

"It wasn't easy, but that's the kind of friend I am."

Lucas laughed again, the sound assuring her that they were okay. Hopefully, more than okay.

"Oh…and, Luc?"

"Yeah? Bootleg Western Wear offered me an endorsement deal."

"Woohoo! Congratulations. I knew that was going to happen. You can tell me all about it on Saturday."

"Yes, it's wonderful, but we have to talk about what that means for the training center." Harper paused. "What it means for…us."

"You have to do what's best for your future. Those endorsement deals are time sensitive."

"Yes. See you Saturday, Luc," she murmured.

She'd dared to use the word *us* and he hadn't responded. Was there an *us*?

Harper sat in the truck a little longer as she realized there were serious decisions to be made.

Should she accept the offer? What would it mean for her partnership with Luc? And what about what she'd glimpsed in his eyes at Dana's party? Had they made a breakthrough, or would she be disappointed again?

Harper rested her forehead on the steering wheel. "Oh, Lord, I have to give all to You, because I don't know what to do."

Chapter Ten

"You saved my daughter's life."

Lucas looked up from his ravioli to meet Colin Reilly's anguished gaze.

For a brief moment, Lucas relived the nightmare of Harper's choking incident. He shook his head to clear the image.

Well, sir, it was the least I could do since I'm pretty sure I've fallen in love with her.

"Heimlich maneuver. First-aid class." Lucas looked from Harper's father to his pasta, unsure of what his next move should be.

"My apologies," Colin said. "My plan was to allow you to enjoy your meal before I spoke. My emotions have gotten the best of me."

"Gentlemen, you aren't eating." Liv Moretti Morgan stood next to their table with a frown on her lovely face. She stared pointedly at Colin. "If that isn't the most delicious eggplant parm you've had in your entire life, your meal is on the house."

Harper's father raised both hands as if in prayer. "My apologies, chef. This is absolutely primo."

"It is." She turned to Lucas and lifted her brows as if to ask what his excuse was.

Lucas scooped up a ravioli. "The best."

"Very good." Liv nodded as a satisfied smile touched her lips. "Enjoy."

For minutes, Lucas was left to do just that. He savored the rich tomato sauce with hints of basil and the pillows of pasta filled with a creamy butternut squash and sage-laced Italian sausage mixture. Bess's cinnamon rolls ruled the world, but Liv's pasta could bring an army to its knees.

Colin wiped his mouth with a linen napkin and pushed his plate to the side. He folded his hands and stared at Lucas thoughtfully. "I'd like to apologize, son."

Lucas finished chewing and carefully swallowed, lest there be a repeat of the choking incident the other night. He glanced fondly at his ravioli, making a mental note to get a to-go box.

"What for?" Lucas eyed the older man nervously.

Harper's father leaned across the table. "I underestimated you. For that, I humbly apologize. You and my daughter are more alike than I gave you credit for. The unfortunate event the other night and a few strongly worded comments from my dear wife have helped me to adjust my attitude."

"Oh?"

"I think you're a fine match for Harper. Joining the Reilly and Morgan family would be a sound plan."

"Joining our families?" Lucas coughed.

He didn't know what to say. One minute he's feeling like he's not good enough for Colin's daughter, now… Well, he expected to hear the details of the dowry. Two cows, three pecan orchards and a tractor would work.

Nice of the man to offer his approval. That almost-kiss the other night was the only inclination Lucas had had that Harper might consider moving him out of the friend zone. And that near miss seemed to be based on emotions riding high.

He'd spent the last few days mulling his relationship with Harper. Could he convince her that they had more than a business relationship?

"I'd also like to invest in your project."

Lucas stared at the man once again. Colin Reilly gave new

meaning to the term "steamroller." He kept talking as though his was the only voice in the room.

"What project is that, sir?" Lucas frowned. One way or another, Colin seemed determined to ensure that anything that touched his daughter would be a success. Apparently, he didn't have confidence that Lucas could do that on his own.

"The business you and Harper are launching. Obviously, I'd prefer my daughter committed to a long-term position at Reilly Pecans. Since the training center is her plan, I'd like to support her. Besides, always good to invest locally."

"Thank you, sir. I'll make note of your interest for our next meeting." They didn't have meetings, but he wouldn't accept any offers until he spoke to Harper.

"Do that. I want to be your primary corporate sponsor. I know you're related to Anthony Moretti by marriage, and cattle might seem like a closer product match, but remember that I spoke to you first. And I am Harper's father. That's even fewer degrees of separation if you two make a merger on a personal level." He winked.

Colin really was bartering his youngest daughter. Harper would be furious if she knew.

Lucas nodded as he spoke, while debating whether he should throw more competition into the mix.

What would Harper do?

He knew immediately

"Actually, sir, I've had another offer for corporate sponsorship." His brothers would love to sponsor the training center. They just didn't know it yet.

"You have?" Colin's brow knit. "How is word getting out so fast?"

"Your daughter does have excellent marketing skills."

"Yes. She does. I ought to hire her." The other man laughed. Lucas chuckled as well.

"Are you going to tell me who the other sponsor is?"

Lucas clucked his tongue and gave a slow shake of his head. "That's confidential at the moment."

"I'll double their offer and go a step further. Harper mentioned that cabin on your ranch. As your corporate sponsor, I'd like to help you renovate the cabin Harper told me about. Underwrite the cost."

"The cabin is already under renovation."

Okay, not yet, but it was on his to-do list.

"I can donate some type of swag with both of our logos. How about pens or mugs?"

"Those have already been delivered. I have more pens than I know what to do with."

Colin's eyes rounded as though both surprised and impressed. "Talk to Harper. Let her know I support you and the business. Especially since it means my daughter will remain in Homestead Pass."

"I understand." Oh boy, did he understand. This meeting was all about keeping Harper close, which was fine by him, except there was no way would he hold her back from the endorsement deal. Clearly, Colin didn't know about that offer.

"Out of curiosity, do you mind if I ask why you chose the Lazy M for this project?" Colin asked. "Seems to me that Harper's property might have been the better choice."

"Harper's property?"

"Yes. The one she used as collateral on the loan application. Probate was completed on her grandmother's estate..." He paused, as if thinking. "Must have been three months ago. That property has better egress and room for expansion. Didn't she suggest Bettie's land as an option?"

Lucas froze at the reveal, working not to give away his surprise at the information Harper had failed to disclose. There was no way he would let Harper's father know he didn't have a clue what he was talking about.

"I, um…she may have, but as Harper probably mentioned, I've lost a few memories in late August."

"Still. We're days from October. I would have thought they'd be back by now." Colin picked up his water and downed the liquid.

"I feel the same way."

"That has to be a nuisance."

"Yes, sir."

"I have a friend who's a top-notch neurologist at a hospital in Texas. Maybe I should give him a call."

"I appreciate the offer, however I'm under the care of a board-certified neurologist in Oklahoma City."

Colin gave a thoughtful nod. "Fair enough."

Lucas's phone buzzed and he pulled it from his pocket. Harper. No doubt offering a get-out-of-jail-free card. It looked to him as though she didn't believe he could handle her father.

He hit Decline.

It took another thirty minutes to extract himself from Colin. On the ride back to the ranch, he mulled over his conversation with the man.

Irritation threatened though he did his best not to jump to conclusions as to why hadn't Harper mentioned the collateral.

Once home, he shoved his to-go box in the fridge and strode to his father's office. He had picked up his glasses yesterday. That meant it was time to read the contract with the bank line by line.

Gramps popped his head into the room about the same time that Lucas finished a first pass on the paperwork.

"Nice glasses. They make you look like a college professor."

"That would be Sam. I'm the cowboy with the memory issues."

"Aw, knock it off. No feeling sorry for yourself."

"No? I don't get it, Gramps. Why couldn't the Lord have

healed me completely and returned my memories? I feel like I'm taking the long way to get to my destination."

"Isn't that why it's called faith? Someday, I trust we can ask Him all those questions. In the meantime, faith and trust go hand in hand." He offered a lift of one shoulder. "Oh, and Harper is here to see Della. I told her to go on down to the stables."

"Thanks, Gramps." Lucas stood and stretched, removing his glasses.

He dreaded the confrontation with Harper, dreaded hearing from her that she had used the land as collateral when she'd known how important it was for him to launch the training center himself. His gaze went to the picture of his parents on the desk, and he sighed.

"Everything okay, son?" Gramps asked.

"No. Everything is totally messed up."

"Can I help?"

"Yeah. Time for a chat with Harper. Pray I can lead with my head and not with my heart."

"I can do that. As I recall, that's a favorite prayer for all you boys." Gramps chuckled. "Remember, when in doubt, close your mouth." He ran a hand over his chin. "I've never found that to be particularly useful for myself, but who knows? It might save your bacon."

"Sage advice, as usual, Gramps."

Minutes later, Lucas found Harper outside Della's stall, talking to Jim.

The sound of his boots on the stables' flooring had her turning. She smiled as he approached. "Della is a beautiful animal."

"That she is. Trustworthy as well."

Jim cleared his throat. "If you'll excuse me."

Lucas barely heard the words as he stared at Harper. She stroked Della's mane while he struggled to push down the memories of how she'd felt in his arms and how he'd thought he might be in love with her. Just looking at Harper had his heart hurting.

Why didn't she tell me about the collateral? He'd made peace with his business becoming their business. This news made the training center one-hundred-percent her business, and she hadn't bothered to tell him.

"I had an interesting lunch with your father."

Harper whirled around, the reddish-brown hair swinging. A smile lit up her face. "No doubt," she returned. "What's he up to now?"

"He wanted to know why we're starting the training center on Morgan land instead of the land you put up for collateral."

She opened her mouth to speak, but he kept talking. So much for Gramps's advice.

"You put up your inheritance. The land your grandmother left you."

"Yes. That's true." She nodded, her eyes wide with concern.

"I don't know what that other Lucas Morgan told you, but I thought I'd been really clear. I wanted to launch the training center without someone else holding me up." He took a breath. "Why your property?"

"Because I don't have a use for it, and it made sense to ensure that the loan went through." She looked at him. "Luc, you came to the realization that we likely were not going to get the loan on our own. We were rejected once. Our options were limited as neither of us wanted to ask our families."

"So you stepped in with this plan?"

Harper crossed her arms. "I decided it couldn't hurt to have the property valued by an inspector. Turns out it ticked all the boxes. Available for residential use. It has a well on the property too." She frowned, her eyes meeting his. "I went over our financials half a dozen times and there wasn't any other way."

"Did I agree to this?"

"Not officially."

"You submitted the paperwork without telling me?"

"I planned to tell you. Over dinner in Lawton. We never made it that far."

"So you decided to keep it from me."

"Decided?" Harper sucked in a breath. "Seriously, Luc?" He recognized her gestures to control her temper. "You said your glasses would be ready this week. Read the contract. It's there in black and white. I didn't hide anything from you."

"I just read the contract. The thing I'm struggling with isn't in print."

"Oh?"

"You didn't tell me because you knew I'd be annoyed. And I am."

"No, I didn't want to push you or stress you, like the doctor said." She huffed and kicked the ground with her boot. "Was I wrong not to tell you sooner? Yes, I can see that I messed up. But deceiving you was not my agenda."

"What was your agenda?"

"There is no agenda. Once upon a time, two friends realized they had similar dreams and decided to work together." She paused. "What a horrible person I am to want to make both our dreams come true."

He scrubbed a hand over his eyes. She didn't get it. Nobody understood why he had to do this himself.

"Luc, using the land for collateral is not the end of the world. It got us the loan, didn't it?"

"Not the way I wanted."

"If I hadn't put up my grandmother's land, we wouldn't have gotten the loan." When she looked at him, he had to look away. "Sometimes you have to compromise. That's what a partnership is all about."

"I don't want to compromise."

Her jaw sagged. "So you'd rather the project tanked than accept my help?"

That wasn't what he'd meant. But to tell the truth, he didn't know what he meant right now. Nothing was working out the way he'd expected.

Harper paced back and forth a moment and then stopped, inches from him. Her perfume mocked him, so he stepped back.

"It's amazing that you can walk with that giant chip on your shoulder and that pride hanging around your neck, weighing you down. I applaud your efforts so far."

Her expression faltered for a brief moment and then her face became red, signaling Harper was full-on angry. "You know what? There isn't room for my opinion in a conversation with you and your ego. From today on, you can consider me your silent partner."

"How can you be a silent partner when you pretty much own the training center on paper?"

"I'm strictly your cosigner on anything necessary to the functioning of the business. Call my attorney when you need my signature." She waved a hand and marched to the entrance doors. "I'm out. I'll be on the road with Bootleg next year anyhow."

"That right? Well, good for you. You earned it." The words were hollow and flat.

"When the business turns a profit, which it will since it's a brilliant plan thanks to me, you can pay off the loan. Eventually, the land will be removed from the title as well as my name. I can always start my own training center on my property."

"Wait. Did you say you have an attorney?"

"That was your takeaway? That I have an attorney." Harper gave a shake of her head as she slipped out of the stables, leaving him standing there alone with the horses.

Della whinnied and stared at him with an accusing glare

as he paced back and forth, trying to figure out how things had gotten so out of control.

"She's right, you know."

He turned around to see his grandfather in the doorway.

"You heard."

"Hard not to." Gramps stepped into the stables. "Lucas, you've let this whole memory thing make you bitter. What happened to the happy-go-lucky grandson you used to be before you whacked your head?"

"Pretty sure that fella is long gone. Not before he spent all my money on swag, a horse and a ring."

"A ring? I haven't heard anything about a ring."

"Never mind. The point is that everything that's happened in the last six months is playing out in real time. I feel like I'm reading the biography of Lucas Morgan."

"Why get angry about the situation? Maybe the solution is to relax and laugh. Nothing you can do about things anyhow."

"Gramps, Harper used her land as collateral for our business. Head injury or not, I would never have approved that move."

"Even if it was the only way to launch your dream?"

"Yes." He paused. "No. I don't know. All I'm saying is that maybe the fella I was before my accident is the real fraudster here." He poked himself in the chest with a finger. "I'm the legit Lucas Morgan."

"That may be so. But, son, you owe Harper an apology. She's an innocent bystander in your battle with yourself."

Lucas released a long breath and shook his head.

"Yeah, Gramps. You're right. But I don't have the emotional energy to do anything else today. It can wait. Maybe Harper and I can find a solution somewhere in the middle of this muck."

"You better pray she's still around when you pull your boots out of that muck."

* * *

A sick feeling settled in Harper's stomach as she looked out at the orchards from her position on the horse. She sniffed back tears that threatened, refusing to allow them to fall.

The vibrations of the hydraulic arms that shook the pecan trees provided a white noise in the background. Harper had grown so accustomed to the sound that she barely noticed it.

Her dad was right. A terrifying thought, indeed. She couldn't spend the rest of her life following Lucas around. Reilly Pecans wasn't so bad, except for the whole desk-in-an-office-with-tiny-windows thing. The pay was good, and she had a flair for marketing.

Maybe she'd sign the contract for the Bootleg Western Wear, stash the funds in the bank and call it quits after she'd fulfilled her year of obligation. She'd have enough cash for a down payment on a house.

A place of her own.

And there she'd be, alone in her house.

Katrina Bednar had given her thirty days to accept or decline the offer. Harper intended to lift the situation up in prayer rather than risk repenting in leisure over a bad decision. There were plenty of doors opening. She simply had to walk through the right one.

Wasn't that what Pastor McGuinness's sermon addressed this morning? "Liminal space," he'd said. The transition place from where we are to what He has for us. "That takes faith. It's not about jumping into our future, it's about being still and waiting."

Harper wasn't very good at waiting or with change. She liked to have the map in front of her with everything laid out.

That's what had made this last week torturous. Not knowing. Not knowing what she should do next. Not knowing if Luc would get his memory back or realize he was a jerk and apologize.

None of this would have happened if Luc hadn't lost his memory. The continued rub was that he still remembered nothing from the last six months. No wonder he thought she'd usurped his dream. It had been their dream once.

Harper slipped off her horse and they walked across the field to the stream that cut through this portion of her father's property. She stood at the bank as the water sloshed over the stones in a frothy haste. The smell of water and tall grass filled the air.

Her phone pinged with an incoming text.

Maybe it's Luc.

She pulled it from her pocket, fumbling and nearly dropping the device. It was not Luc.

You have to stop. Luc is over. He's never going to feel the same way about you as you do about him.

The text was from her mother. A reminder that chef would have lunch ready in fifteen minutes. Harper typed back that she'd be there shortly. She wasn't hungry, but it would behoove her to show support for the newest hire as it kept her mother out of the kitchen.

First, she'd call her friend Jackie about her invitation to the rodeo and the wedding. Harper punched in a number. "Jackie?... Yes, it's Harper... I'll be in Tulsa next Friday. You have yourself a date for the wedding."

It was time to get out of Dodge and clear her head. Harper smiled. She'd mark today on her calendar. Her father was right and now she recalled her mother's words. *Go. Have fun. You deserve a break.*

Yes, Mom was right as well. She'd been walking on broken glass for two months since Luc's accident. The last few days she'd functioned by rote, driving to Reilly Pecans and home again. Hardly eating or sleeping, living on coffee while trying to figure out how everything she had banked on had fallen apart. The thing was, she couldn't fix it. That was the real issue.

Her entire life, she'd been an overachiever, determined to do things herself and not rely on her family name. She'd succeed, too, by being strong, goal-oriented and focused. It had gotten her a scholarship for college and a successful career in rodeo. But it couldn't get her what she wanted most.

For her best friend to see that they had a shot at a future together. Yes, if the last six or so weeks had taught her anything, it was that she couldn't make Lucas Morgan love her.

Chapter Eleven

"You sure you're supposed to be doing this?"

Lucas grabbed the keys for the UTV off the wall of Trevor's office and turned to face Slim Jim.

"Yeah. Didn't I say so?"

The doc had okayed him to drive yesterday and recommended short distances to start with. Lucas strode to the vehicle. It was Friday, the sky was blue, and his brothers weren't around. The construction on the training center had paused while the crew allowed the concrete to dry.

It was a perfect day to work on the cabin.

He'd convinced Jim to pick up a load of lumber in town for him, so he didn't have to answer any nosy questions. Now, they transferred the 2 x 4s from Jim's truck to the UTV.

"Where you headed with this lumber and those tools?"

"To the cabin on my parcel."

"Sam's a carpenter. Have you thought about asking him for help?"

"Ever thought about minding your own business?"

Jim transferred another 2 x 4. "Sure are a lot of cranky people around here lately."

"That implies more than one."

"Yep. I can count. You and Harper. The woman nearly bit my head off at the barbecue party 'cause I wouldn't dance with her."

"Harper? That was weeks ago."

"And you can see I am still traumatized." He pulled the circular saw out of the truck and put it in the UTV. "I'd have gladly taken her for a spin. Since I won that line dancing competition last year, word of my skill on the dance floor has spread. But I turned her down out of loyalty to you, my friend."

"Loyalty to me?" Lucas stopped what he was doing and looked at Jim.

"You're in love with her. Any fool can see that. Why, at Trevor's wedding, you hardly let her out of your sight."

"That was two months ago and, for the life of me, I cannot remember any of it."

"That's a problem. You sure acted like a man who lost his heart to a particular woman. That's all I can tell you."

Lucas shook his head. Had he been in love with her at the wedding? He couldn't help but think about the pretty diamond in his duffel bag. Could the ring be for Harper?

How was he going to find out?

"What are you thinking about so hard?" Jim asked.

"Nothing and everything." He looked at his friend. "She asked you to dance."

"Sure did, and that woman has a temper. Let me tell you. My plan is to never get on her bad side again."

Yeah, she did. Harper didn't get angry often, but when she did, look out. She made a rodeo bull look timid.

"Well, I appreciate the information and the concern for my safety."

"But you're still going out to the cabin by yourself."

"Yep. It's time. I've been sitting around for weeks. I couldn't lift anything because the doc didn't want me to mess with the pressure in my eyes. Couldn't read because it gave me a headache. What did that leave me? Six weeks of doing nothing. Bess felt so sorry for me, she let me make cinnamon rolls the other day."

Jim's jaw sagged and his eyes bugged out. "You saw the secret recipe?"

"Focus, Jim. I'm saying I need to do some physical labor."

"I see your point. A fella needs to work with his hands. It's therapeutic.

"Therapeutic. That's one way to look at things." Luc saw it as an opportunity to burn off his anger, but therapeutic was good.

He couldn't remember going into business with Harper against his better judgment. But, apparently, he had. Willingly.

Why was it only now that he'd discovered his partner owned the collateral which was foundational to the entire business? So much for doing it on his own. The center ought to be called Reilly Training Center because it sure wasn't a fifty-fifty operation. Nope, Harper was the real owner.

The thought chafed and embarrassed him.

He ought to be grateful to have a partner as committed as Harper.

She hadn't told him about the collateral on the loan. That's what kept looping through his mind over and over. Why hadn't she told him?

"I can stick around and help," Jim said. "Not much going on today."

"Huh?" Lucas turned to look at his friend.

"I volunteered to help you."

"The idea is for me to be alone."

"Oh yeah, sure. I get it. Man against the land." Jim dusted off his hands and nodded. "Sure hope the man wins."

"Thanks, pal. Good to have your support."

Waving Jim off, Lucas headed to his parcel. He parked the UTV near the cabin, got out and took a slow walk around the construction area. The crew hadn't wasted any time. Concreting of stub columns was in progress. He didn't know much about construction, but Drew sent him updates.

Returning to the cabin, Lucas pulled the lumber from the vehicle and tossed it on the ground. Then he got a crowbar out. First, he'd deal with the steps and then the remains of the railing had to go.

He maneuvered around the hole in the steps from Harper's near fall and two-stepped to the cabin door. When he turned the handle, it wouldn't budge. Lucas pulled hard, using his booted foot as leverage on the frame. It popped open.

Something leaped at him, causing him to stumble backward. Something big. A huge daddy of a raccoon. At least a thirty-pounder.

Grabbing the remaining railing for support, he avoided tumbling to the ground. A good move as it kept him from landing on his head. His neurologist would likely have frowned upon that. Instead, both his feet crashed through the landing floorboards and his arm hit a broken piece of railing.

Great. Wedged in and unable to free himself. He recalled when Harper had fallen through the steps. If he tried to pull his legs out, he would certainly cut himself on the edges of the wood that spiked like shards of glass.

Lucas yanked a bandana from his pocket and assessed the gash on his left forearm before awkwardly wrapping the scrap of cotton around the arm and tucking the ends in neatly. It wasn't like he was going to bleed out, but there was no point risking an infection.

Grabbing his phone from his pocket, Lucas debated who to call. It had to be someone discreet. He'd like to keep this incident from getting to his brothers.

He couldn't call Harper. Bridges had been burned there. Maybe Jim was still around.

A moment later, a rustle in the woods behind the cabin caught Lucas's attention. He prayed the raccoon hadn't returned for round two.

A horse and rider appeared.

"Looks like you have a problem," Trevor said from astride his mare.

The sound of an engine had Lucas looking in the other direction. Sam and Drew pulled up in the other ranch UTV.

"Good timing, I'd say." Drew grinned as he slid from behind the steering wheel. "What do you think, Sam?"

Sam's smile was even wider, with a little I-told-you-so mixed in. "I say that if we're going to do this, let's do it right. I brought tools."

Lucas grimaced. So much for keeping this from his brothers. "How did you know I was here?"

"Jim might have mentioned it," Trevor said as he dismounted. "Said he smelled trouble. We should probably promote him from horse whisperer to trouble sniffer."

Drew laughed at that. He reached for a hand saw in the back of Lucas's UTV.

"Whatever," Lucas said. "He's off my Christmas list for sure."

"Don't blame Jim. He might have saved your life." Trevor approached the steps and frowned. "What happened?"

"I'd tell you that a raccoon jumped me, but then you'd laugh. So I'm not answering on the grounds that this is going to be a story for the next dozen Sunday dinners no matter what I say."

Now all of his brothers were laughing. "You got that right," Drew said. "Be grateful we didn't bring Gramps along."

"There is that." He'd never hear the end of it from his grandfather.

"What did you do to your arm?" Trevor asked. "You and that raccoon wrestling?"

"Real funny."

"I'm starting to think Mother Nature doesn't like you. Those broncs stomp on you more often than not. A deer tackled your truck. Now a raccoon."

"It's a small cut."

"That bandana says otherwise. I have first-aid kits in the back of the UTVs courtesy of my wife, the RN. I'll grab one."

Sam approached the steps with a handsaw. "Don't say I never do anything for you." He knelt on the ground and proceeded to cut Lucas out of the broken boards.

"Thanks," Lucas said as he extracted one leg then the other and slapped at the dust and dirt on his jeans and boots.

Trevor removed the bandana, cleaned his laceration and dressed the wound.

"You're a pretty good nurse," Lucas said. "Got a mean mug, but your heart's in the right place."

Trevor eyed him unsmiling. "I used butterfly bandages, but you need to head to the clinic for a few stitches."

"I'll do it when I'm done here." Lucas held up his right arm where a row of scars from an incision trailed from his elbow to his wrist. "A few stiches are nothing compared to last year's accident. This can wait a few hours."

"Stubborn," Trevor said.

Sam shook his head. "Prideful."

"Hardheaded," Drew added.

His brothers formed a semicircle around him.

Lucas backed up, but they continued to move closer. "Is there something you want to say, fellas?"

"Yeah. There is." Drew pointed at him. "This gotta-do-it-all-yourself attitude is getting old."

"We're a team," Sam added. "Teamwork is what teams do."

Teamwork. Hadn't he just said that to Harper? Harper, who he'd practically kicked out of his life. Oh, the irony.

"Luc, we're like the five musketeers," Drew said. "The Morgan brothers and Gramps. All for one and one for all. We've been that way since the folks passed. You gotta stop trying to do it on your own."

"He's right," Sam said. "We're standing on the shoulders

of giants at the Lazy M. Those are Mom and Dad's shoulders, and we're nothing without each other."

Emotion clogged Lucas's throat. He nodded and hung his head.

"We're family," Trevor said. "You and I are twins, and you still won't let me in unless it's on your terms."

Lucas released a breath and dared to look at Trevor. "I've leaned on you and Drew and Sam all my life. You were the ones who held me up when Mom and Dad died. Those days when I all I could do was cry."

"You cried," Sam said. "So what? We made a big mistake with our stoic responses. Trying to be strong because Gramps lost his only child." He sighed. "Gramps didn't need us to be strong. He needed a distraction from his pain. He needed to be needed. Maybe you were the only one that got that right. You were the one who helped Gramps get through that time."

"We're all we have in this world," Trevor added. "Each other. The Morgan brothers. Don't lock us out, Luc. We want to be part of your world."

Each of his brothers gave him a man hug. Though they avoided eye contact, he knew they were as glassy-eyed with emotion as he was.

"Come on. Let's get this cabin in shape," Sam said. "A couple of meetings of the Morgan boys and it will be like new."

"What are you going to use it for?" Drew asked.

"You know all those pens, hats and mugs I bought before my accident? This cabin is going to be where we sell training center merch."

"That's a great idea," Trevor said.

"Harper's idea."

"Of course it is," Trevor returned. "She's the brains of this operation."

Yeah, she was. The brains and the heart and soul, and he'd

ruined everything by letting his pride get in the way. His brothers had made him see that.

The sun had begun to set by the time they stopped for the day. The steps and the landing had been replaced. Next time, they'd tackle the rest of the porch and the railings.

Once his brothers left, Lucas stood and stared at the cabin, admiring their progress. They'd managed to restore what had been damaged. Could he do the same with his relationship with his best friend?

Lucas got in the UTV and headed to the barn. His phone rang and he quickly reached for it, praying it was Harper.

Not Harper.

He stopped the vehicle and answered.

"Morgan here."

"Mr. Morgan, this is Amy from Keller's Family Jeweler in Lawton. We spoke a few weeks ago. I'm sorry to bother you so late in the day, but I do have news."

"You have information on my purchase?"

"In a manner of speaking. We've found your order, and it seems we owe you a refund. You paid for engraving on the ring and never received it. I'm so sorry for this oversight. I can send you a check, or if you would like to bring the ring in, we'd be happy to add the engraving."

"Engraving? What engraving?"

"Give me a moment to find that." She paused. "Ah…yes. Here it is. 'LM & HR. Best friends forever.'"

Lucas's jaw dropped and he slapped the steering wheel, his heart beating against his chest. *Harper.* All this time, it was Harper.

"Are you there, Mr. Morgan?"

"Yes. Yes. Sorry." He paused, collecting himself. "Thank you. This means a lot."

"Do you want to stop by and complete the engraving or shall I issue a refund?"

"Truthfully, I'm not sure. I have your number. I'll get back to you."

"That's fine. Again, I'm so sorry about this inconvenience."

"Inconvenience. This is nothing, ma'am. It's all good."

All this time, he'd been fighting his feelings for his best friend, and somehow, even with his memory gone, he'd known she was the woman he wanted to spend the rest of his life with.

Lucas tamped back his pleasure at the discovery. There was nothing to be happy about, yet. Harper could very well be on her way to the first stop in her Bootleg tour by now.

His throat tightened as he punched in her number on his phone.

The call immediately went to voice mail.

Desperate, he called Maureen Reilly.

She picked up on the first ring. "Luc, how are you?"

"Not so good, ma'am. I've messed things up, and Harper isn't answering her phone."

"Well, that explains so much." Maureen paused. "Harper is loading up her truck right now. You better hurry. She's leaving for Tulsa shortly."

"Can you stall her?"

"I'll do my best. How far away are you?"

"Twenty minutes."

"We've got this, Lucas." He could hear the smile in her voice.

"I sure hope so." Lucas ended the call. "Lord, I'm going to need some help here."

Harper looked at her phone. Nearly a week since her argument with Luc and he decides to call today. Nope. She was not picking up. A gardenia could not fix what was broken. The bond of trust between them had been destroyed by his failure to trust her.

She'd cried her eyes out for too many nights before she realized it was time to get away from Homestead Pass, clear her head and spend some alone time, praying about what came next.

"Harper, have you seen my car keys?" Harper closed the tailgate and turned around. Her mother stood on the front portico in jeans and her artist's smock.

"No. I never drive your car."

"I've an appointment. Could you please help me locate them?"

Harper cocked her head and assessed her mother's clothes. "You have a Friday night appointment?"

"I do."

"What's your appointment?"

"Does it matter? I need my keys."

"Fine. I'll look for them." She glanced at her phone. "But I have to get on the road soon."

"Thank you. You know I wouldn't ask if it wasn't important."

"Let's retrace your steps. When did you see them last?"

"Hmm. In the kitchen, I believe."

"Okay, I'll look in the kitchen. You check your purse."

"I'll do that."

Harper muttered to herself as she searched the kitchen countertops and drawers for ten minutes. Her mother was a brilliant artist who functioned like an absent-minded professor when she wasn't in her studio.

The new chef entered the kitchen as Harper rummaged around the utensil drawer. "What are you looking for?" she asked. "Maybe I can help."

"My mother lost her keys."

The woman pulled a set of keys out of her pants' pocket and dangled them in the air. "These?"

"Yes. Where did you find them?"

"In the refrigerator."

Harper snatched them. "This is another reason why we

never let my mother in the kitchen. Thank you." She glanced at the wall clock and raced out of the house.

"Found them," she called. When she got to the portico, she saw Luc standing next to the Lazy M Ranch pickup. She stiffened. No. No. No. Her heart couldn't go another round with Luc.

"What are you doing here?"

Her mother took the keys from her. "I'll let you two chat."

Harper's gaze went from Luc to her mother. "Did you plan this, Mom?"

"I wouldn't say that. Would you, Lucas?"

He offered a somber nod. "No, ma'am. This was all my idea."

Harper shook her head, confused. "What are you doing here?"

"Talking to you, I hope."

She glanced at the truck. "You drove?"

"Yep. All doctor approved."

She stared at him, uncertain what to do. His hair was damp, as though he'd just showered, and he sported a large bandage on his left arm. "Your arm?"

"My dumb pride got in the way." He put his hands in the pockets of his jeans. "Could we talk?"

"What do you want to talk about? How I tricked you into starting a training school and provided collateral to make it happen? Or maybe how I'm taking over the business you didn't want me to be part of in the first place."

"Guilty on all counts." He released a pained breath as his gaze raked over her. "Harper, let's forget about the training school. Close up shop right now."

"What?" She sputtered, searching for a response. "It's your dream, Luc. Besides, we already spent some of that loan."

"I'll use my truck money. I'll sell my horse. Whatever it takes." He pulled his hands from his pockets and raised them

as if pleading. "I want to go back to the way things were...
The way I don't remember."

"That doesn't make any sense."

"Sure it does. I've messed things up, and I'm here to say
so. To apologize. You're right. I let my pride and my ego put
a wall between us. And I need to explain."

Harper sucked in a breath. She wanted so badly to believe
him, but she couldn't go back to being his buddy.

"I don't know..." she began, her attention on the tips of
her boots.

"Please, Harper. Give me one more chance."

Raising her head she saw something in his eyes that gave
her pause.

"Go ahead. Explain," she murmured.

Lucas ran a hand over his face and cleared his throat. "I
didn't know you when my folks died. It was a tough time and
I struggled. My brothers... Well they've always been protec-
tive of me because of it." He hitched a breath.

"Oh, Luc." She stepped toward him, and he moved back.

"I gotta finish now. I've kept this inside too long."

Harper nodded, holding back tears for the young boy who'd
lost so much.

"When I planned the training center, I figured it would be
my way to show my family that I had what it takes. That I
could do it myself." He cleared his throat and met her gaze.
"I was wrong. I can't do it alone. I need my brothers and the
Good Lord and..." He cleared his throat. "I need you."

"I can't go back to the way things were," she whispered.
"Because I want more, Luc. And I think you need to figure
out what you want."

"Oh, I know what I want. I just told you. I want to go back
to the moment I knew in my heart that you are the one I want
to spend the rest of my life with. I might not have my memory
yet, but I put enough of the pieces of the past together to fig-

ure it all out. Turns out, the other Lucas is a lot smarter than I gave him credit for."

He pulled the ring box from his pocket. "You're the reason I went out and bought a diamond engagement ring. Losing my memory made it take a little longer to figure it out. But I finally did."

"A ring? What are you talking about?" Stunned, Harper licked her lips as she stared at the box in the palm of his hand.

"This ring has an interesting history. Apparently, I bought it for you. Not that I recall buying it or anything."

"How do you know that?"

"The jewelry store called me and told me."

Harper opened her mouth and then closed it, her thoughts racing.

"Is it too late?" Luc asked.

"I…" She blinked, her gaze on the ring box. Was this really happening?

"I fell in love with you twice, Harper. Doesn't that give me bonus points?"

"You love me?" Her heart soared at the tenderness in his expression.

"Yep. Twice. The first time was before I lost my memory. I didn't want to wait to start our life together. I knew you were the one before we'd even had a first date and that's why I bought the ring."

His eyes searched hers as he continued. "These last weeks since the accident, I've fallen in love with you all over again. How could I not? And, by the way, I plan to get the ring engraved this time. In case I hit my head again and forget I love you."

"You love me?" He kept saying the words she'd never expected to hear.

"Of course I do. Who else would put up with me? I finally understand why the other Lucas wanted a partnership."

"That's the nicest thing you've said to me since you lost your memory."

He laughed. "That's not true. I just said I love you."

"I love you, too, Luc. I always have."

"That's because you're smarter than me." He got down on one knee and opened the ring box to reveal a sparkly marquise diamond.

Harper looked from the ring to Luc. Her heart began to stutter, and her hands trembled at the love shining in his eyes. Luc really did love her.

"Will you marry me, Harper Reilly?"

"Oh, Luc. Yes."

Lucas stood and slid the ring on her finger, though she wasn't sure how since she was shaking so hard. He put his arms around her, and his lips met hers.

"I love you, Harper," he whispered.

"I love you, too, Lucas Morgan."

"Please, just tell me you aren't going to get married at a rodeo."

Both Harper and Luc turned to find her mother on the portico, smiling.

"Mom, you have got to stop eavesdropping."

"That's the thanks I get for losing my keys." She rushed down the steps. "Let me see that ring."

Harper held out her hand and laughed. "Isn't it beautiful?"

"Oh, Lucas," her mother said. "You have excellent taste."

"That's the truth." His gaze met Harper's. "Would you excuse us, Maureen? Harper and I have some planning to do."

Harper waited until her mother had left and then she turned to Luc. "What planning?"

"I plan to tell you a few more times how much I love you."

She laughed and pulled his head down to hers. "I love you, Lucas Morgan."

Epilogue

Lucas sat in the bleachers of the Gus Morgan Jr. Arena with Harper. They'd started a ritual of praying together each morning since the training center had opened in the spring. Each day, they took their coffee and Bibles to the site and prayed for the instructors, students, and the horses.

There was a beautiful peace to the arena this time of day. Today the scent of smoke from fireplaces mingled with the crisp smell of fir trees. His favorite perfume. Each morning, he thanked the Lord for all that had been given to them.

The chute sign advertising Reilly Pecans flapped as a breeze passed through. Lucas turned at the sound. His gaze spanned the fencing surrounding the arena, taking in dozens of colorful vinyl banners. The most prominent sponsorship banner featured the Lazy M Ranch. Lucas smiled at that.

He would raise the American flag and the familiar blue flag of the State of Oklahoma on the tall flagpoles once prayer time had concluded, officially starting another day.

"It's going to be a busy one," Harper said. As usual, they were on the same wavelength.

He nodded. Yes, tonight, the last graduation of the season was scheduled. Students enrolled in bronc-riding and barrel-riding training would circle the arena, stirring up the red dirt to entertain the crowd who filled the stands to watch their loved ones before they were awarded certificates of completion.

Harper zipped up her jacket and inched closer to him as the sun rose higher in the sky. The mornings were nippy as winter threatened to make an entrance. They would have to move their prayer time to the inside arena soon.

Opening his thermos, Lucas poured more coffee into his mug. The aroma wound itself around him. He took a long sip of the warming brew before closing the thermos lid. "Our first anniversary is coming up in a few weeks."

Harper stretched out her hand and admired her engagement ring nestled next to a white-gold band. The delicate marquise diamond seemed to wink at him as if to remind him of the day he'd purchased the ring. A day that he still couldn't recall.

Lucas shook his head.

"What?" Harper asked.

"I sure would like to remember buying that diamond."

"It doesn't matter. What matters is I'm the only gal whose cowboy fell in love with her twice." She looked up at him and sighed.

Lucas leaned close enough to touch his lips to hers. "My Cinderella," he whispered.

Harper put her arm through his. "Things have certainly changed in the last twelve months."

"You mean the fact that neither of us has been outside of Oklahoma since I asked you to marry me?" he said. "Do you regret not taking the Bootleg offer?"

"No. My days of wandering are over. This is where I want to be. With you. All my dreams are here. All my tomorrows."

"Mine too. How do you want to celebrate our anniversary?"

"I thought we could have a party like Dana did."

He groaned. "Tell me you're not serious."

"Not in the starter castle. We can use the indoor arena, hire Moretti catering, and invite all our friends and family."

"Like my exes party."

"Yes, but without the exes or the hors d'oeuvres."

"Sounds good to me."

Harper shivered as a breeze passed by. She pulled the wool cap on her head down around her ears.

"Want a sip of my coffee?" he asked. "It's hot."

"No, thanks." She wrinkled her nose.

Luc reached into his backpack, pulled out a container and popped the lid to reveal plump cinnamon rolls slathered with cream cheese icing. "Bess hid these for us."

"I'm going to pass. My stomach is a little queasy."

"What? No cinnamon rolls?" He frowned. "Maybe you should schedule an appointment at the clinic."

"Oh, I've been. The doctor tells me that it's nothing nine months won't fix."

"What?" He turned to her, confused.

A mischievous smile lit Harper's face and her green eyes sparkled. "Do the math, Lucas."

He blinked. "We're having a baby?" Joy bubbled up inside as he processed her words.

"It turns out we are. I know the timing is all wrong. The doctor recommended I stop riding when I hit my third trimester. This is definitely going to throw a wrench into our spring programming schedule."

He started laughing. "The best kind of wrench, Harp."

"I know we talked about starting a family after the business hit its second year."

"We're having a baby," Lucas murmured. "We have a nursery at the house from when Drew and Sadie lived there. Of course, we'll have to head into Oklahoma City for supplies. We'll need a high chair and a car seat for starters."

"Did you hear me?" she asked. "About our programming schedule?"

"I did. I absolutely did." He couldn't stop smiling. "Wait until Gramps finds out. This will be his sixth great-grandchild. Six. Imagine that."

"Yes, but what will we do about the training center?" She pulled out her phone and began to scroll through her address book. "I could make a few calls. Find a replacement. Jackie said she was interested."

Lucas put his hand on hers. "Harper, relax. Everything will work out. We're going to trust the Lord. Like we always do."

He pulled out his glasses and opened his worn King James Bible. He flipped through the pages until he found 2 Samuel 22:33. "'God is my strength and power: and he maketh my way perfect.'"

"Yes. You're right," Harper murmured. "Absolutely perfect."

He brushed his lips against hers. "We're having a baby."

* * * * *

Dear Reader,

I hope you enjoy the conclusion to the Lazy M Ranch series. It's been so much fun to see the Morgan family grow into a large extended family who serve the Lord and have filled up every seat around the kitchen table.

Lucas and Harper's story was especially fun because of the Cinderella twist. What did you think?

Also, I have good news for those of you who bake. Since this is our last visit to the Lazy M Ranch, Bess Lowder has agreed to share her cinnamon roll recipe. You can find it on my website under the Blog tab, along with a few more recipes from this book. You'll also find recipes from the first three Lazy M Ranch books there. Email me at contact@tinaradcliffe.com if you need assistance.

Thank you so much for taking this journey to Oklahoma and the Morgan brothers' ranch with me. I'm going to miss Drew, Sam, Travis, Lucas and Gus.

Sincerely,
Tina Radcliffe